CW00864860

20/20 Vision

They didn't see it coming

Sue Miller

Sue Miller was born in London and has lived most of her life in the north east of England. She has spent many years as a teacher, psychologist and senior manager developing and delivering services for children and families. She has worked in areas where individuals have experienced the challenging social, economic and environmental changes that local and national governments, as well as communities, have sought to address. As a university lecturer she has written extensively on parenting, childhood, care and education and the complex leadership and learning issues involved in managing and adapting to ever changing circumstances. She is married and has two children.

20/20 Vision: They didn't see it coming is her first novel

For Seve

The most wonderful and the strongest things in the world, you know, are just the things which no one can see.

Charles Kingsley, *The Water-Babies*

Acknowledgements

It's generally friends and family that most of us turn to when riddled with self doubt. You are the ones who keep us going, convince us we have something worth saying, to be brave, stop messing about and just say it. You know who you are. This book would not exist without you.

And Keith, who just reminds me every day that the only thing that really matters is to love and be loved.

September 16th 2098

Light crept into the cottage and Anna stirred. Her dreams hung like vapours, caught in threadbare flannelette sheets rumpled over a lumpy mattress. For a blissful moment she experienced the feelings she had had every day for the last few months, genuine surprise and thankfulness to see another dawn. As she got thinner her bones were becoming more pronounced. She knew what Erin would have said if she had still been alive: *'Better to face facts my dear. None of us goes on forever. What doesn't kill you makes you stronger.'*

Sighing half in her head, half out loud, she grunted and, with an effort, shuffled her legs out of the bed. She picked through tumbled clothes and slipped out of her thick pyjamas. For every aspect of dressing that was challenging she had a series of well worn techniques to get the job done on her own. There was some satisfaction in that at least.

A grandfather clock in the corner stood beside a lead paned window with dusty tapestry curtains. Five a.m. It was time to go. Pulling on a coat and lifting the latch on the wooden door of her ancient cottage she felt the air on her face, damp and heavy with overnight rain, as she emerged into the grey dawn.

At the sound of the door a young woman appeared at the window of the neighbouring cottage and Anna's heart skipped a beat, as it always did when she first saw her niece in the morning. She could never quite get used to just how much she loved her.

Raising a hand in greeting she wrapped her arms around herself and rocked from side to side, sending a hug across the space between them. 'Happy birthday!' she mouthed.

With a wave, the young girl smiled an acknowledgement and a few minutes later tumbled through the door and hugged Anna with ready familiarity and uncomplicated affection. A black and white collie trotted at her side. She snapped her fingers and waved the dog forward to Anna's door.

'Come on Lela. You're staying with Seb today.'

The dog obediently trotted into the cottage that Anna shared with her son. Once she was inside the girl closed the door behind her.

'I'm ready.'

'Got the food?'

Lucy rolled her eyes, slapped her hand to her forehead and ran back into her house emerging with a wicker basket which she heaved into the cart.

'Uh huh.'

Anna flashed a warm smile, taking her niece's face in both her hands and they momentarily nuzzled noses before she tousled her hair.

'Good job I'm here! Let's go.'

The horse the two families shared was already hitched to the light cart standing in the yard. Heaving herself up onto the seat, Anna expertly steered through the narrow gap between the two cottages and turned to the left, heading for the road south out of the

2

village and across the causeway to the mainland. They quickly left the shelter of the high wall that acted as a boundary to the road and moved out into a space that would soon, with the turning of the tide, become open sea. From a short distance the sound of waves reached them rolling rhythmically, crunching over the sand bar and across the beach that stretched north and south into the distance. Settling comfortably against the wooden upright, both women wrapped their coats tightly to their bodies to protect themselves against the early morning chill.

Dark navies and pale silver light were gradually separating sky from sea and land. Willow trotted briskly through the silent village, the clattering of hooves and sound of wheels over cobbles echoing loudly. They passed the dark shapes of trees and cottages looming out of the half light. Within a few minutes they had reached the causeway linking the Community to the mainland. There they were hit by the sharp, tangy and unmistakeable smell of the open sea.

The tide was moving in fast and in places the carriage splashed through seawater puddles that were already forming on the sand. Wooden stakes marked the path of the causeway that stretched from the island all the way to the mainland. They were ancient relics, planted generations before by travellers from a different time. Men and women who, like them, had once trudged across the shingle in search of a place of peace, and had reached what was now their island. They had probably contemplated the same views that the two

3

women could see today, views that had barely changed in a thousand years.

A few seabirds whirled high above them. Anna urged the pony into a swift trot and it took only a few minutes to traverse the stretch of land being rapidly metamorphosed by the incoming waves.

At the crossroads she swung the carriage southwards, her eyes constantly turning to the sunrise in the east. The road rose in a steady gradient. There was not a breath of wind and the air, even at this early hour, felt full of the promise of a dry and beautiful autumnal morning.

Anna smiled at the sight of her niece leaning forward and looking eagerly into the distance. Everything about Lucy spoke of youthful optimism: she was almost singing out loud with eager anticipation for the day ahead. Anna recalled an expression her father used to use when he was feeling positive and refusing to be downhearted about life. He would have called Lucy '*a glass half full.*'

The sound of horse and carriage settled into a steady rhythm, the dawn light gradually bringing clarity to familiar landmarks. They pointed these out to each other as they went along. A huge elm topped by a tangled mess of twigs. A rook that rose lazily, floating high above the fields before it disappeared into the distance. Spiders' webs that spangled with dew shimmering along hedges. At one point Anna caught sight of rabbits breakfasting on moist greenness at the roadside ahead. They scattered as the carriage approached, flashes of brown and white disappearing into the undergrowth. Lucy spotted a heron gliding in to rest on nearby wetland.

They made good headway along what had, at one time, been a main artery, linking a string of villages dotted like beads along the coastline. Some had been real jewels, large enough to support homes of character with high streets housing whole communities. They passed a farmhouse, perched up on a hillside overlooking the road. From there a view stretched far out across the sea in one direction and in the other extended to rolling fields and farmland. It was clear from the abundance of vegetation that the land was rich and fertile, but everywhere it was dishevelled, eerily silent.

Eventually they came to an old Iron Age site, now not so much a jewel and instead little more than a shiny pebble. Animal bones, cooking utensils and other evidence of a settlement dating back thousands of years had once been unearthed there. It was a link with the past. A time that could not in some ways have been more different, but where so much had been the same: people eating, sleeping, and making a life together.

Anna grimaced. 'Don't know what they'll make of my back kitchen in a few thousand years.'

Lucy giggled. 'Well, they'll know we don't waste much, that's for sure.'

The sun rose, a huge orange pumpkin floating over the horizon. Anna pulled off her hat and let the light breeze created by the forward movement of the carriage play through her hair. As the air grew warmer Lucy unbuttoned her coat and loosened the next

5

layer of uncoordinated clothing she had bundled on in the semi darkness when she had woken. It was a glorious morning.

Reaching under the seat, Lucy pulled out an old and very battered ukulele. Resting it on her lap she started to strum a few chords, stopping every so often to tune it carefully. Willow's ears twitched and she almost danced forward to the notes with renewed vigour. Once Lucy had the tuning settled she broke into the opening lines of an ancient but familiar folk song that she had been teaching herself. Both women started to sing as she plunked out the rhythm, laughing as they each tried to remember the words.

'It's strange,' said Anna 'we know every word of the chorus, but have no idea of the verses.'

'They're always the same anyway. Crazy stuff about loving dodgy men who pop their tin whistles, with a fal laddy diddy and a fal diddy doh,' laughed Lucy.

Anna shoved her playfully 'Hey, not so much of your cheek! I happen to like a bit of whistle popping! And besides, they bring back loads of memories these songs. Your Mum and I used to sing them all the time with your Gramps when we were little. He loved them.'

Anna set a steady pace along the road. The view was breathtaking. Leaves whirled to the ground in playful dancing bursts. Trees dotted along the roadside wore their colours with unconscious beauty. They reminded Lucy of big, fat roosting birds, ruffling and fluffing glistening layers of feathers every shade of amber and russet. As they passed under one, a beech leaf floated down and fell on her lap. It was perfect, a smooth spine and veins, golden brown and spotted with yellow. She stroked it gently before letting it slip through her fingers and drift away behind her.

All around them hedgerows were bursting with fruits, red hips, bundles of elder, blackberries at different stages of ripeness, rich and darkest purple, others still red and raw but holding a promise of the sweetness soon to come. Crows circled above them and every so often they would see one tucking in to some carrion it had found either in a field or on a roadside.

Looking around them, as Lucy strummed, Anna sighed contentedly at the beauty of the world. On a day like this you could almost believe that all was well.

Every so often they passed evidence of previous human habitation. Small cottages were dotted individually along the roadside, as well as being clustered in what must once have been thriving communities. But it was obvious this was no longer the case. The villages looked sad and neglected. Vegetable patches had been overrun with weeds. The houses themselves were still standing, but in various stages of disrepair and dilapidation. Unloved, Nature had long since started the process of reclaiming the land for herself. What had been and still bore the faded signs for churches and farms all along the roadside looked, truth be told, not that much different from how they might have done fifty years previously. But their surroundings had not stood the test of time well. They passed roads that had not been repaired, trees that had blown down, and fences that had fallen. There was no sign of anyone up and about, but the impression left by the landscape went deeper than that. There was no sign of anyone at all.

The Gift

Having been on the road for about an hour they crested a hill and came to the site of an old wind farm. There were three giant structures each with blades like bronzed arms that had once turned slowly in the breeze. They loomed above them, their obviously human fabrication making them appear out of place in the rural landscape. Silent, ominous and foreboding, belying their original benevolent intention to provide the power to enable communities to survive, now they were anachronisms from a way of life that Lucy knew had existed but could not begin to imagine.

As the sun rose steadily and the miles slipped by, the conversation of the two women turned to their destination. The lighthouse where they were heading was one of the only buildings left standing along the coast, visible because of its height from afar and attracting anyone who was travelling northwards away from the worst ravages of the south. Several people who were now part of the Community had first made contact by meeting Anna and Lucy there. The two women made regular visits, fitting them round the other responsibilities that they each held for foraging and farming. Whenever possible they brought back those that had not, after a period of quarantine, shown signs of anything contagious. This had helped to swell the Community's population to its current level.

At first there had been a steady trickle of arrivals. They amounted to refugees; people escaping northwards from the flooding, diseases and pollution that had developed following a series of catastrophic global disasters, some arguably predictable, others unforeseen. More recently numbers had dwindled to almost nothing. The women's trips had become routines of low expectation, managed disappointment and resignation.

That was why they had been so thrilled on their last visit to find the children. It had been almost a week ago. There were two, an older girl who said she was twelve and a little boy, Sam, her brother, who was five. They mentioned their parents and some other family members who they had travelled some of the way with but said they had '*got lost*.' Anna and Lucy, as was the custom and practice of all the Community, did not probe. They knew only too well that, whatever their history, it would not be one on which the children would want to dwell.

Lucy sighed and broke the silence. 'It was so tough to leave them. I just wanted to bring them straight back with us.' She stared pensively out onto the road ahead, and then down at her hands, picking at a hole in the knee of her leggings.

'It's not fair.'

Anna nodded. 'I know, love. But rules are rules.'

As a mother herself, it had been especially hard. All of her instincts had screamed stay, look after these children, they need you. But those voices had been stifled by a sense of responsibility to the Community, whose health could not be risked by possible contamination. So, they had kept their distance, let them into the old lighthouse keeper's cottage and dropped off the food supplies they had brought, showing them the fishing lines they could use and where from the rocks they had the best chance of catching a meal. They told them they would return in a week. If they were still healthy and presented no signs of any of the viruses which their Community had become so familiar with over the years, then they could join them.

Leaving had been tough. Forced to ignore the cries of the little boy, they had each also had to find a way to deal with the woeful and accusatory looks of the girl. Anna had explained to her the situation. She was old enough to understand, surely? The pair needed to stay isolated to give a chance for their health to be assessed when the women returned.

'I don't think she liked it when I said to be brave and responsible, to take care of her little brother like a grown up,' said Anna.

Lucy nodded ruefully. 'No, you're right, she didn't.'

The road had risen steadily but now it began to flatten out, its elevation giving them a view across to the sea that was glistening in the distance. Anna pulled gently on the reins and the cart slowed to a halt. Everything went suddenly quiet. There was just the sound of the wind rustling the leaves and Willow's jingling bridle and snuffling breathing.

Dropping the reins and turning to Lucy, Anna placed a hand on her shoulder and drew her closely to her. After a few moments she pulled back and held her at arms' length.

'You're growing up yourself now,' she said. 'Sixteen. I can't believe where the time's gone.'

'I don't feel grown up really. Well, sometimes I do, but sometimes I don't feel any different from when I was little.'

'Me neither,' Anna laughed. 'I still feel sixteen, and I'm nearly fifty! One thing's for sure, I'm not getting any younger!'

They sat for a moment in companionable silence, and then Anna seemed suddenly to make a decision. Reaching into her pocket she drew out a piece of cloth and placed it in Lucy's hand.

'Lucy, this is something very special for you for your birthday. It belonged to your Mum. She wanted you to have it. I promised her I'd give it to you when you were sixteen.'

Taken off guard, Lucy gasped. Unwrapping the cloth carefully, she revealed a silver necklace bearing a small round pendant. She remembered her Mum wearing it. The pendant was finely painted, with a stencilled outline of a black oak tree showing its roots going deep into the ground. Above the image were two words: 'Grow Strong.'

The silence hung between them, a heavy black shadow casting a sudden gloom where only moments before there had been sunshine. Lucy gently stroked the pendant. She hurriedly rubbed the back of her sleeve across her eyes and nose.

'I miss her so much.'

Anna hugged her closer. 'We all do, love.'

The two sat, gazing across to where the sea and the sky met in the distance. Lucy sighed deeply. Still looking at the pendant and turning it over in her hand, she finally broke the silence.

'I still don't understand why she did it. I could have looked after her. I wanted to.'

'I know you did, love. You're bound to be angry and upset, that's only natural. But she did what was best.'

'Not best for me! Best for her more like.'

Anna's face darkened. 'You can't say that, Lucy, that's not fair. Your Mum would have done anything for you.'

'So why did she do it? Why did she choose to leave me, leave us all, when she could still have been around for me?'

'She had to. She wasn't going to get any better; she was only going to get worse. And she didn't want to be a burden on you.'

'On me? She could never have been a burden on me. On the Community more like.'

The silence descended between them again. Eventually Lucy broke it with a barely audible whisper.

'It's not fair. Why did she have to leave us?'

Anna knew what the Community would say. *Erin: you have become a passenger.*

'It's not fair, Lucy, but there's nothing we could have done for her. What she did was right.'

The words were a detonator, triggering emotions only just below the surface. Lucy leapt to her feet, eyes wide and tearful as she jumped out of the cart scattering the pendant and faced Anna square on, her face contorted in rage.

'Giving up? Letting herself be put down, like a dog? How can that ever be right?'

Anna clambered down, grabbed her niece by the shoulders and shook her fiercely. Then as Lucy started to sob she tried to pull her to her, but she wrenched away and stood, back turned, hands clenched, shoulders heaving with the effort to stay in control. Anna reached out to touch her but she flinched away.

'I don't want to talk about it.'

And with that Lucy climbed back into the cart and, taking up the reins, turned it so that Anna had to scurry to get up into the seat she had now vacated. They had gone just a few yards when she pulled up suddenly, ran and scooped up the pendant, then jumped back in and sat, hunched forward, her eyes fixed on the road ahead. For the next few miles not a word passed between them.

The Arrival

After a couple of hours of travelling they could see the lighthouse in the distance, pointing heavenwards from its small rocky headland and standing out against the clear blue sky. Like the island where the Community lived, it too was only accessible at low tide. Eventually the carriage reached the edge of the raised manmade causeway and they could see that this was now fully underwater. It would be late afternoon before it would reappear.

Lucy looked at her aunt who also had her eyes firmly focused on the lighthouse ahead of them.

'I'm sorry, Anna. I didn't mean it.'

Anna took Lucy's face in her hands and smiled gently. 'I know why you're angry, love. Anyone that's gone through what you have would be.'

Biting her lip, Lucy blinked hard and swallowed. The tremor in her voice when she did speak was unmistakable.

'I can't help it. I know Mum didn't want to be a burden. But she was *my* Mum. She was meant to be there for me and I would be there for her. It just feels like she chose to put the Community first. And I think it always will.'

It didn't seem like there was anything else that could be said so they didn't try. They were impatient to get onto the island, but all they could do now was to wait for the tide to turn again and the way to clear.

Anna unhooked Willow from the trap to graze on the grass along the edge of the headland. They were all three hungry and tired. Reaching into the basket tucked under the cart seat, Lucy took out the bread, cheese and carrots that they had so carefully made and grown on the island. The vegetables she fed by hand one by one, stroking the horse's soft face and resting her head against her flank. She tipped some water from a stone flagon into a bucket that stood next to the pathway and the horse drank thirstily.

Sinking down into the grass, Anna lay back and watched through her fingers as a few stray clouds scudded past while Lucy wandered restlessly up and down, skimming pebbles over the water and flexing her arms in the sunshine. After a while she sat on the grass and the two women slowly worked their way through the bread and the cheese, gazing at the island, trying to pick out any signs of life. When they had finished Lucy stood and, brushing the crumbs from her skirt, shielded her eyes as she scanned the area below, behind and around the lighthouse.

She could see no movement, no movement at all.

Nothing was said. But a feeling of foreboding was creeping imperceptibly over both women.

'I'd have liked to be able to see them,' said Lucy eventually. 'They'd surely not have wandered off the island? We told them again and again to wait till we got back.'

Anna tried to feel positive. They had counted out seven pebbles for the children to use to mark the passage of time. Not much of a game, but it had been the best they could come up with to encourage them to wait till they came back. There was nothing they could do now till the causeway cleared. Lucy carried on pacing. Anna lay back on the grass, closing her eyes and allowing the sunshine to soak into her skin, relaxing into its comforting warmth.

Her mind turned back to her sister's death. Had it really only been a year? She missed Erin, obviously in a different way but almost as much as Lucy did. She had always been there somehow, a strong, protective, big sisterly shield sheltering her from danger.

As it turned out, Erin's shield proved very brittle. The end had come swiftly. Her whole auto immune system had gradually shut down. She had tried to stay as healthy as she could through carefully monitoring what she ate, but that was difficult with so little food to choose from. With no medication to help, her body had grown thinner and weak. She had not been able to work and she could not care for herself. She could no longer contribute. In the eyes of the Community she was redundant.

The end had been exactly as the Community decreed, painless, peaceful, a swift draught of poison distilled from berries and fungi in a concoction as old as time itself. Every part of the process had been designed to emphasise the gift she was giving by voluntarily allowing her life to be taken. Even in death her body, like everyone who passed from the Community, was put to good use. The neat rows of fruit trees growing in the churchyard with roots stretching deep into the well mulched and richly fertilized soil where she had been buried testified to that.

Lucy had been so young, but then so was her mother. Anna had promised Erin she would take care of Lucy but at the same time do everything in her power to protect and nurture her fierce independence and resilience. Heaven knows she would need those characteristics if she was to survive.

The air was warm. Lucy had stopped pacing and was flung out in the grass facing the sea, her head pillowed on her arms. She looked, for once, peaceful.

As Anna watched the clouds she wondered, as she had many times, what it must have been like to live in a community with the freedom and the resources to support you till you died naturally. But that was the past, a foreign country, one that they were never likely to visit. She allowed herself to focus on the rhythmic sound of the waves lapping against the shoreline and before she knew it, like Lucy, she was asleep.

The Recovery

With a start Lucy awoke. The sun had passed behind some clouds and the heat of the day had gone. Her aunt was stretched out on the grass, breathing deeply. The causeway was almost clear.

Jumping to her feet, Lucy called to Anna and then started to run, her scarf a kite tail streaming behind her. It was only a couple of hundred metres to the lighthouse but it seemed much further. She reached the steps that led up to its base and frantically scanned the rocks for movement. Nothing.

She turned towards the cottage where they had left the children, picking her way over the rocks and pebbles strewn across the pathway. As soon as she pushed open the door the smell hit her and she gagged.

The inside was in semi darkness, curtains closed. A movement in one corner drew her attention. As her eyes adjusted to the light she saw the boy. He was curled up on the old sofa, a blanket pulled around him, staring at her from huge eyes.

Trying not to breathe the acrid air, and stumbling in the gloom, she made her way to his side. Dropping to her knees Lucy did what she always did, forgot rules and worked on instinct. She reached out to the child and gently and tenderly took his hand. It fluttered in hers, dry and parchment like, cold. Stroking his hair from his eyes she felt his forehead. No fever. Her heart was pounding from running and she tried to contain her rising fears, not wanting to scare him. He was, after all, very young.

'What's happened?' she whispered. Where's your sister?'

It was a huge effort for him to speak. 'She's gone, miss.'

Anna arrived panting, took in the scene and saw it was too late, too inhuman to hold back. Instead she knelt too and wordlessly put her bottle of water to the child's cracked and dried lips. They both listened as he drew deep gulps into him with sounds that seemed to reverberate around his chest as if it were a drum. Bit by bit he sobbed out the tale.

While trying to fend for themselves, and to get food by fishing as Anna had instructed, his sister had become trapped on rocks on the far side of the island. Unable to save herself, she had been swept out to sea. Alone and not able to keep warm or to find anything to eat or drink Sam had done what he had been told to do, stay in the cottage and count each of the seven pebbles until the 'kind ladies' would come back for him.

At the news Lucy collapsed like a bird shot down mid flight, curled in a quivering ball. And then, not tears, but a wordless requiem rose from deep within her, first gently and then with more insistence. The sound echoed round them, rebounding off the ancient flagstones and dark walls.

Reaching under the blanket, Anna gently lifted the child and cradled him on her lap. His head rested on her shoulder. She could feel a faint pulse trembling through the blanket. Whimpering, he wrapped his free arm around her and lay almost motionless in her arms.

Looking down into his upturned face Anna realised, with absolute certainty, that they would not be returning the present to the Community that she and Lucy had so hoped for and talked about all week. But she also knew they could not leave this little one alone at the lighthouse. He expected a family, they had promised him that. It was his right and their duty to give him one.

Unconsciously Anna had started to rock too, holding the child as close to her body as she could, making comforting sounds of reassurance. After a while his breathing slowed and she knew he had fallen asleep. Gently she laid him back on the sofa, arranging the blankets as best she could and smoothing his forehead.

The two women stayed where they were, their heads bowed together, each of them contemplating what might have been. Lucy remembered something her Mum had once said to her: *'the saddest words you will ever hear are if only...but too late.'*

After what seemed an age Lucy rose and made her way back outside into the gathering gloom. To the west the sky was dipped in pink and orange and she could hear the sound of the waves rolling in over the causeway, trapping them on the island. The world could be so beautiful and full of promise. Why did things so often have to work out like this?

Eventually, when she could not cry any more, she rose and turned back to the house. She went inside and closed the door behind her. A few moments later the flickering of candlelight was just visible through the closed curtain as the gathering darkness rolled in from the sea.

The Homecoming

They stayed with Sam all night, trying to make him as comfortable as they could. Both women slept fitfully, waking every hour or so to listen to his shallow breathing. In the early hours of the morning Anna took his hand and held it in both of hers, willing him to stay with them but suspecting he would not. She lay her head on her arms and found herself whispering a kind of prayer out loud into the void, hoping and pleading for a miracle, but knowing deep down that this was pointless. It would be easier to put him out of his misery. She knew only too well that there were some who would.

Eventually she must have fallen asleep to the sound of the waves rolling against the rocks. When she woke, he was gone. She sensed it straight away. His little body was completely still. His hand limp in hers had no pulse. Lucy started awake, looked at Anna who shook her head. His face shone palely luminescent, frozen in time. They each kissed him gently on the brow then, lifting his arm, tucked it under the blankets. He was finally at peace.

They responded intuitively to what they felt they had to do. At first light Anna gathered him up and they carried the child slowly back across the causeway. Laying him gently on the floor of the cart, they adjusted the blanket so he was hidden.

The journey back could not have been more different from the one they had made the day before. The weather now showed the other side of autumn. Clouds scudded across the skies, the wind beating in their faces and rocking the cart as Anna urged the pony forward. They just wanted to be home. They would bury him in a place that would, eventually, be planted with fruit and flowers. In their hearts they felt he deserved at least that much from them.

By the time they were back to the village it was dark and they were almost asleep, hands and feet numb. The horse found her own way to their cottages. As they clattered into the yard Anna's door flew open and Seb, Anna's son, ran out. Anna sat motionless, her face in her hands. He stopped in his tracks.

'Mum, Lucy! What's happened?'

As Lucy sobbed out the story Seb helped her and Anna down from the cart and into the cottage, doing his best to comfort them.

But Lucy was inconsolable. 'It's our fault. If we'd stayed with them, or brought them back and hidden them, they'd both be alive.'

'It's not your fault,' said Seb.

Holding his cousin in his arms, he could feel the sobbing shaking her whole body. When she finally went silent he held Lucy away from him and spoke slowly and clearly.

'Listen to me. He's not going to be used just for fertiliser. He's going to rest in peace.'

So it was that under cover of darkness, with only the faint glimmer of moonlight to guide them, Anna, Seb and Lucy crept from the cottage and, braving the weather, dug a shallow pit in a secluded corner tucked away under some hedges that ran round the church. Sharp thorns clawed at their clothes, scratching their hands and arms like knives, the pain on their flesh serving to dull some of the anguish in their hearts. Standing by the unmarked grave in silence, arms around each other, they each said their goodbyes in their own way. Sam's body would decay and only they would know it was there. If they were seen they would be in trouble for wasting a resource, but for once they didn't care. Anna summed it up in a quiet murmur as they tiptoed home slowly through the lightly frosting night.

'We all die one day. Maybe there's some comfort in having done something to make a difference with your life.'

'Even if it's just by feeding the soil where you lie?' asked Lucy bitterly.

Anna stopped and took each of Lucy's hands in hers. She could barely speak for the lump in her throat and, even if she had been able to do so, she had no idea what to say. The whole episode had left her confused and upset, but she was the grown up. Lucy and Seb were both looking to her for guidance. What should they have done? Finally she said:

'No matter how painful it is for those left behind, we all need to believe that someone, somewhere will mourn us when we're gone and that we're missed. We're at least giving him that.'

Lucy thought about her Mum and Sam as she fell asleep that night. What Anna seemed to be saying was very simple: whoever you were, when you were gone what mattered was that you left a fond memory in someone's heart. At least that was something her

Mum had done. And what was the other thing she used to say was important? Ah yes: *Make sure you do no harm.*

September 15th 2099

Scrunching up her legs Lucy yawned, stretched and slowly put them, one at a time, out of bed.

A whole year had passed and once again it was autumn. The weak silvery light was finding its way through chinks in thin curtains at tiny windows. Wincing in the cold she slipped her feet into animal hide slippers lying on the hard, uneven stone floor next to the bed. Padding across to the window, she pulled aside a worn curtain and looked out onto the pathway in front of her cottage.

Anna was dimly visible in the watery early dawn. Wrapped in layers of clothes, she had a soft woollen hat pulled tight round her ears. She was about to climb into the seat of a horse and cart standing across the lane. Lucy tapped on her window and waved. Hearing the sound Anna turned and, seeing Lucy, waved back and mouthed '*Good luck.*' Lucy smiled. Her aunt settled into the seat on the cart, took up the reins and, with a flick and click urged the horse down the lane towards the sunrise. Lingering for a few moments until the cart turned the corner Lucy enjoyed the sight of silver and gold in the sky as light streaked in from the east. She could see the features of the lane, the shadowy outlines of the houses, the roofs and walls and gardens gradually coming into focus. '*Even if no one's there, Anna should have a good trip to the lighthouse,*' she thought. '*It's going to be a fine day.*'

Going to the embers in the grate, Lucy gradually coaxed the fire back to life with the poker hanging by the side. She used small twigs, blowing gently and was rewarded by a bright flame as they suddenly caught and flared. Carefully and expertly she added some larger pieces of wood until there came the sound of a crackling fire emitting instant warmth. For a moment she paused, enjoying the heat that always accompanied this first awakening. Coming slowly to standing she felt the familiar early morning pressure on her bladder and walked over to the door, lifting the latch and putting her feet into some old wellingtons that had been deposited on the threshold. As she did so, a black and white collie lying curled in a basket by the door, raised her head, stretched and came to her to be petted.

'Morning, Lela.' said Lucy reaching down to fondle the dog's ears and then cradling her chin in her hands. 'Mamma's Big Day today. We'll go and see Jude and see what he's got for us.'

Crossing the small yard Lucy used the toilet in the outhouse. Looking around at the whitewashed walls she reflected, as she always did, on those that had been there before her. '*Not the first and certainly not the last,*' she sighed as she scattered a thin layer of earth down the hole in the water closet.

She made her way quietly over in a few steps to a dark shed in the corner of the yard. Lifting the latch, she peered into a henhouse where half a dozen dozing birds were gradually rustling and moving in response to her presence. Ducking her head, she slipped inside. She loved these birds like they were family, knew each one of them inside out, their different personalities and characters. She could not bear to think that one day any of them would end up in a pot and had hatched any number of escape plans for them, each more ambitious than the last.

'Hiya lovelies,' Lucy cooed, letting the door drop to behind her. 'Let's see what you've got for me today.' And with great care she gently searched in the straw, pulling out a total of three warm, freshly laid eggs, one white and two brown, each with a fine freckling of dark amber spots.

Walking back to the cottage she stood for a few moments in the tray of precious disinfectant next to the doorway, taking a long slow intake of breath, trying to absorb the mixture of smells that greeted her. She ticked them off in her mind: the sharp acidity of the disinfectant, the coolness of the late autumnal morning air, the dampness of the grass and seaweed wafting in from the shoreline. This was her world.

Once back inside, Lucy selected a rough glazed blue bowl from a shelf by the sink, carefully put the eggs into it and set them on the table.

She dressed hurriedly. Stooping to look in a small mirror, the end result showed an emphasis on keeping warm, being practical, comfort. Lucy surveyed her reflection in the mirror and grimaced. *'I look like Mum,'* she murmured. Half unconsciously she reached for a small silver pendant with an image of an oak tree hanging over the bedstead and slipped it over her head. She lifted it to her lips, and reading the inscription gave it a tight squeeze and dropped it to her chest.

Turning from the fire and collecting a pan of water from the rain bucket outside, Lucy made herself a mug of mint tea using herbs she picked from ones growing in a wooden trough at the window. Rabbits hung in the pantry off the kitchen and swayed gently as she closed the door. She ate her breakfast, savouring every mouthful, the white egg she had just brought from the hen house and some bread kept in an old fashioned bread bin, white and blue enamel with a lid, chipped but still functional. She chose the egg with care, weighing each of the three one by one in her hands and deciding to leave the brown ones for later. 'Anna and Seb'll like to share those tomorrow' she said to Lela.

Sitting at the table, Lucy watched the dawn break over the island. Lela contemplated her attentively, her eyes never leaving her face. Once finished, Lucy brushed the crumbs from her hands, tossing the bread crusts to the dog who snapped them up appreciatively.

'Come on girl. We'd better be going. Can't keep Jude waiting.'

Reaching up to the hook behind the door Lucy took down a brown woollen coat and, pulling it on, prepared to leave the cottage. She placed a kiss on her fingers and touched a faded photograph of a woman hand in hand with a man propped on the window ledge next to the door. A jar of wild flowers sat next to this. A certain shrine like quality to the area contrasted with the mismatched functionality of the rest of the room. As Lucy and Lela left the cottage a petal dropped from one of the flowers and landed on the sill. Stillness settled over the scene as the first bright shafts of sunlight seeped into and illuminated their home. It now just had to wait, and would embrace them again on their return.

The Beginning

It was only a short walk to Jude's cottage. He was the Community's Chief Steward and she had been summoned yesterday to appear before him. Lucy felt herself being drawn reluctantly along, torn between a desire to get the meeting over and done with and wishing that she didn't have to go. Anna and Seb had both promised to support her in whatever Jude was going to ask of her, but she could still feel her heart beating faster as she got closer.

In the distance she could just see fields of corn ready for harvesting and passed a whole line of men, women and children walking determinedly off in that direction. Every so often a woman or older child passed her carrying a baby or leading a toddler by the hand on the way to a slightly larger cottage standing near the centre of the village square. It had a walled garden and, as she passed, the door opened and a young girl aged about fourteen hurried out and headed off up the path, looking to catch the contingent making for the fields. She nodded to Lucy as she passed

'Hi Scarlett. How you doing?'

'I'm late,' the girl stopped momentarily. 'Fin wouldn't settle this morning, but I've had to leave him crying.'

'He'll be alright,' said Lucy, reassuringly. 'I won't hold you up. You don't want to let the others have to get started without you.' And with a brief nod and smile the girl turned the corner and hurried away towards the fields.

Lucy regularly took a childcare shift at the cottage, as did all the young women over twelve and any of the older Community members who needed a break from manual labour. She rather enjoyed it, telling stories, playing games, teaching skills that would be useful to the children once they were old enough to take their place in the workforce. Fin was one of her favourites, bright eyed, fiercely independent but always ready when he was tired to snuggle into 'LouLou,' sucking fiercely on his fat little thumb as he slipped into sleep.

She passed people on bicycles, some driving horses and carts all intent on the tasks ahead but nodding and greeting each other by name as they set off for these. She knew that further out in some of the small holdings and farms there would be people taking cows for early morning milking. Later in the day the youngest children would be sent up the lanes to fetch milk in jugs and cans for the evening meal. All being well, there would be just enough to go round.

This was a simple Community, very different from the world of her grandparents. Lucy knew that, in theory, by joining it she had become a survivor, one of the lucky ones. But sometimes that wasn't how it felt.

She soon reached Jude's cottage. Lifting the heavy knocker she let it drop with a dull thud. There was the sound of a chair being pushed across a hard floor, steady footsteps and a low screeching of metal on metal and a latch being lifted from within.

A thin figure, dressed in a brown habit and monk like in appearance, stepped forward into the greying dawn light. Piercing blue eyes fixed on Lucy and the man placed his pale hands on each of her shoulders. She could feel a slight tremble running through Jude's body as he gently pressed down, holding her in his grasp.

'Welcome Lucy. Come in.'

Jude stood aside and with one hand moving to the small of her back firmly but deliberately propelled her across the threshold and into the room.

Once inside, Lucy paused, unsure whether to take a seat or to stay standing. Jude sensed her hesitation.

'Sit here Lucy,' and he indicated a low chair set against a dark wall on which hung a simple cross. The morning light filtered through the criss-crossed lead latticed window opposite, illuminating her face. As the sunlight intensified, she felt uncomfortable and was forced to move to avoid being blinded, consciously pressing her hands into the seat so as not to reveal that they were trembling.

Jude took his place in the large, high backed chair opposite, a cold empty grate leading to an open chimney between them. His face was shadowed. His hands rested half curled, palms down on the chair arms. Gently moving them back and forth, stroking the smooth patina of the wood, for a few seconds he carefully studied Lucy's face and then allowed his eyelids to fall and shut off his gaze.

A period of silence settled over the cottage. Lucy felt her breathing quickening. This always happened when she was in Jude's presence. His stillness unnerved rather than calmed her, but she had no idea why. The more he appeared contemplative the greater became her desire to spring, run away, bolt.

She took a moment to glance around the room. It felt very different from her cottage. Row after row of manuscripts, neatly ordered, cataloguing every aspect of the Community's life stretched from floor to ceiling. It was the work of an ordered mind, of someone who valued details, data and personal histories. As she ran her eyes over the shelves, noting the neat handwritten script on the labels on each tome, Lucy could not help wondering, as she had many times before, how anyone had the time or why they would want to record so much.

Opening his eyes, Jude raised his hands and placed them palm to palm, prayerfully in front of him, his elbows resting lightly on the chair arms. He gently tapped the tip of his long slender nose with thin, almost skeletal fingertips. Lucy felt she could see watery blood flowing through them under a pallid yellowy tinged skin. As his eyes focused on hers she found herself sitting up straighter, such was the quiet authority of the man.

He took a deep breath and, as he exhaled, spoke in a soft low voice, resonant with gravitas.

'It is good to see you, Lucy. Thank you for coming. Shall we get down to business?'

She nodded. In one short phrase Jude had managed to clarify so much between them: boundaries, relative purpose and function, roles and status. For her, there was still only the vaguest outline of understanding about the reason for her summons this morning. But she was gradually realising she was there to be given instruction.

This was typical of Jude. In a way it had been a relief when they had first arrived on the island not to have to think for themselves. Once the family had realised that the place they had always called home was no longer viable, they had travelled northwards like so many others, sensing this was where they had the best chance of finding land capable of supporting any sort of living or population.

When she had first met Jude she had initially thought of him as kindly, grandfatherly, someone who would act diligently and steadily, be reliable, not rock the boat, conform. As she had got to know him better over her time in the Community Lucy had realised that she had probably underestimated him.

His attention to detail and ability to remember the smallest incident had at times caught her off guard. She had seen how it had also sometimes startled, but also engaged fellow Community members when he recalled dates that might be meaningful to them: a birth or death, a natural occurrence like a storm or flood that had made a significant impact on a family. She glanced again at the files, each with scrawled names cataloguing family histories, some with red crosses on the spines. She wondered what that indicated. *'He must study those a lot,'* she thought.

She and Jude could not be more different in personality. Her Mum had always called her an open book: *'You are incapable of hiding your feelings Lucy.'* And she had never been one for obeying people in authority at the best of times, something that had frequently got her into trouble with her parents. *'You'd never make a soldier,'* her father used to laugh. *'Your favourite word's 'Why?' We should have called you 'Bother'. You're such a pain in the butt.'*

If success in a battle was about unswerving obedience her Dad had been right, she would make a terrible soldier. She always had to challenge, ask questions. She had to admit she quite liked being a thorn in the flesh sometimes. *'If that's what it takes to get noticed,'* her Mum used to say to her Dad, *'then that's what she has to do.'*

As far as she was concerned just being old did not mean you were necessarily right.

'Let's face it,' she had once said wryly to Seb when they were out foraging together for food from a long deserted neighbouring village, 'Grown ups don't know everything. We probably wouldn't be in half the trouble we are now if they'd had a bit more sense.'

The Interview

Jude stroked his hand over his neatly parted, greying hair as if smoothing it into place, though there was no need. He was immaculate. He looked intently at Lucy. She felt rather like an interesting moth being studied under a microscope.

'How are you feeling, my dear? What is the state of your health?'

Jude always spoke in these measured tones. They befitted his status. His words were, on the surface, inconsequential, the concerned grandfatherly enquiry of a fellow member of the Community. But coming from Jude they held a different intent, or at least she perceived them that way. He was the Chief Steward after all. It was his duty to know the state of every member of the Community's health: mental as well as physical and emotional. However, knowing the importance that he would attach to her response made it impossible for her to give an unguarded or wholly truthful answer.

'Alright, thanks,' she replied and paused. This was so hard. Her natural inclination was always to spill out her feelings and emotions, her fears and anxieties.

'You look tired. It was good of you to come so early.'

Lucy felt instantly patronised. Part of her wanted to relax into his apparent kindliness and embrace it as sincere interest, rather than condescension, but she knew that could never happen. Maybe it was not entirely his fault. Nothing Jude said or did could ever really be separated from the role and responsibilities he bore.

He seemed to sense her discomfort and, smiling benignly, changed tack. 'We have much to do today. But first, please allow me to offer you some refreshment.'

He stood, and moving to the table poured some water from a large earthenware jug into two small wooden bowls. Passing one to her he waved his hand towards a dish containing small berries that looked recently gathered from the hedgerows.

'Please, eat, and as we share these simple fruits of the land together I will explain why I have called you here today.'

Cupping one of the bowls in her hands, Lucy sipped at the cool water, finding it soothing to her dry throat and then rested the bowl on her lap. She left the berries. Although at a quick glance most appeared familiar, there were some amongst them that she did not recognise. She was sure Jude had been around long enough to know which were safe and which poisonous. But there were often stories of individuals reacting badly to unfamiliar tastes and her Mum had always impressed upon her not to take any risks with anything gathered from the countryside.

Jude remained standing. Turning his back to Lucy he stretched out his arms and rested his hands on each end of the mantelpiece above the empty grate, grasping it like a lectern. He bowed his head, appeared to gather his thoughts and then slowly turned to face her. The light was intensifying, finding its way through the small windows set like eyes in the face of the wall on either side of her host. She could not make out Jude's features, but the sunlight glinted around the outline of his body, for a moment appearing to make him shimmer.

'You have lived long enough in the Community now to understand our challenges, Lucy.' He paused dramatically. 'You recognise, better than most, the sacrifices we all have to make to survive, the consequences for our loved ones of the limitations of our resources, both natural and in ourselves.'

Lucy could feel her heart throbbing. She tried to appear calm, breathed deeply and swallowed hard. She could not trust herself to raise the bowl of water to her lips and instead grasped it tighter. If Jude noticed she was trembling he did not show it. He was watching her closely, but his eyes were impassive.

'Lucy, as I'm sure you can see I am not getting any younger. I need to look to the future and prepare for that. One day I will require a successor, someone who will take on the responsibility of leading our Community, especially our young people. We have almost five hundred souls living here now, but that is not enough to maintain our existence in the long term. Young people are the future of the planet. There is no way of us being certain, but we may have to face the possibility one day that, because of the current state of the world, those of us who are here are the only ones left capable of sustaining a Community.'

The words hung darkly in the silence. Jude took a sip of water and cleared his throat before continuing.

'As you are aware, everyone in the Community has a strong sense of duty. Nothing is wasted. We recycle, we are frugal. We have rationing in place for all elements that are basic for life: water, food, land, materials, fuel. We lose loved ones of course. But we also reproduce and have new births, a source of great celebration.'

'We work as a team, as one family essentially. But we are still a long way from being safe, Lucy. Our gene pool is very limited which as you know is why we have to think so hard about our responsibilities to reproduce. Our resistance to disease is easily compromised. We need to continue to focus on preserving the healthy and creating children who will be strong. We need more people who are capable of being productive.'

Those words were delivered with real intent. Doing your duty in the Community extended to every choice, even who you bore children to and how often.

'There are always events we just can't stop. No one really knows, for instance, how dinosaurs were wiped out. We can't be sure whether lack of sunlight or a virus played a part in their demise. And just before you were born we saw unexplained increases in the Sun's activity. Solar winds drove particles with higher energy towards us. During one particular 24 hours they caused the whole world to experience an extraordinary episode of shimmering colours in the night sky. But those particles also seriously damaged communication satellites and triggered massive power cuts across continents. The hidden effects, however, were much more serious. Far more of these particles than usual were able to reach the earth's

41

surface and, as they passed like a tsunami through the bodies of unwary onlookers. We now know they caused significant damage to human cells.'

'Now we suspect it would only take one bad harvest, one rogue disease and we could lose everything we have worked so hard to achieve. We who remain are vulnerable. There is no place for the selfishness of valuing one more than another just because they are a relative or a friend. We have to take the long view.'

'Yeah, you don't have to tell me,' Lucy retorted. She was only too well aware that the cost must never outweigh the benefit any individual brought to the Community as a whole. That was what Jude said was fair. But she hated balancing the needs of the few over the so called wants of the many, especially when you found yourself or someone you cared about on the wrong side of those scales.

Jude nodded emphatically.

'Yes, my child. We need more people. But it's a balancing act. The Community is too fragile to be able to carry passengers.'

Lucy shifted uncomfortably in her chair. She hated that word.

Noticing her unease, Jude paused. Closing his eyes again he appeared to be searching for a way to justify his position. Then he looked directly at her.

'This is how I would explain it, Lucy. Throughout history there have been cataclysmic events that no one could have prevented but that have changed the planet beyond recognition. However, that does not excuse us from our responsibilities to manage those aspects over which we do have some control. We are caretakers, stewards of the planet. You could say that we are the victims here and that lack of effective action in the past has added even more problems to a terrible hand. Whatever the reason, we have been left a huge responsibility to manage.'

His tone became bitter and for the first time real anger and emotion crept into his voice. 'My parents and grandparents said they cared for me, but for all their lobbying they seem to have been ineffectual in changing the thinking of people that made the big decisions. Those individuals were short sighted, failing to address effectively the way humans were destroying huge parts of our planet. The evidence was all around them of the impact of their actions, but there were too many self interests and distractions. Multi-national companies seemed to have had far too much power and influence. Leaders failed in their responsibilities to take action at a global level. Do you not think that I rail against the injustice of the sacrifices all of us, you especially, have had to make as a direct consequence of their inability to take strategic decisions for the benefit of all?'

The Steward's face was flushed. He had spoken with rare passion. Lucy felt suddenly faint. The wooden bowl she had been grasping rolled across the floor as she dropped forward in her seat.

Jude stood up and crossing in front of the fireplace, knelt before her. When she lowered her hands from her face he wrapped his around them and held them steady till her body had stopped shaking. They were smooth hands, but clammy. To her surprise she noticed that all the nails had been chewed down to the quick.

'I know this is hard Lucy. We cannot solve everything, but we have to learn from the past. It is not enough simply to say we care. We have to be responsible, to act. Your great grandparents said they cared, but to me they appear at best naive and short sighted, at worst selfish and lazy. They said the words, but too often they failed to act, to take the hard decisions, make the difficult choices that at least would have protected the world's natural resources. They left us weak and vulnerable with their mess to sort out.'

'We want this cup to pass from us because what it contains is so bitter to swallow. But instead we have to deal with it. I believe that is our duty.'

Lucy stood up. 'I'm sorry Jude, I need some air,' she mumbled, and avoiding the wooden bowl lying upturned on the floor she opened the door and stepped into the bright morning sunshine.

Once out in the square, Lucy breathed in deeply. Standing with her face turned up to the sky she allowed the warming rays of the sun to fall on her skin, her hands fisted by her sides. She wished Anna and Seb were with her.

After a few moments she could sense her head clearing and feeling coming back to her fingers. Turning, she saw Lela lying patiently by the door, watching her attentively. She crossed to her and nuzzled her ears with her hand, smoothing her head and back. Then their eyes met, a look passed between them and, in that instant, she understood what had to be done. With a sigh she straightened up and pushing open the door, she went back into Jude's cottage.

Duty Calls

The wooden bowl had been returned to the table and refilled with water. Jude was now sitting at the head and Lucy crossed to a chair to one side.

'I'm sorry,' she said.

Jude nodded. 'It is understandable, you do not need to apologise. This is not the life any of us would have chosen.'

Lucy sat, but Jude remained standing. When he next spoke he sounded more human, as if very weary. He must, Lucy reminded herself as she reflected on the conversation that night, after all be easily seventy years old.

'I have tried to work out what is going to help us all. That is my duty as Chief Steward. It's the responsibility that has been laid on my shoulders when you chose me for this role.'

Jude spoke slowly and carefully.

'Lucy, if we are to rebuild we have to sustain and increase our numbers somehow. But they have to be the right numbers. I have a plan for a Project which I have named 'Duty Calls' which I believe will maintain the viability of our Community. Will you help me to make it happen?'

She was taken aback and hesitated before answering. 'That'll all depend on what you want me to do.'

'Of course. Let me explain.'

As he spoke, Jude paced back and forth across the room, as if giving a speech on a platform.

'For some time now, and because of the limitations of our resources, once we are judged more costly as an individual to maintain than the contribution that we can make then we can choose to have our lives ended medically but humanely.'

He paused. 'Even our deaths make a contribution to our sustainability. Our bodies are buried rather than cremated and we are thus recycled back into the food chain.'

Lucy thought of her Mum and the boy she, Anna and Seb had buried secretly a year before and shuddered.

'If euthanasia is the Project then Duty Calls is a terrible idea. I hate it.'

Staring intently at his hands and gently rubbing them together, Jude looked thoughtful. 'This idea of making choices and taking control of the timing of our deaths and the designing out of poor genetic material is not new, Lucy. Quality of life debates abounded in our grandparents' and great grandparents' days as medical capabilities pushed the frontiers of what was possible.'

'Yes, but then you got to choose who you had children with or the time of death yourself, or at least your family did.'

'Not always. There were never enough kidneys or hearts or livers to go round. Once science allowed it, people very quickly started to design their babies and make a choice about what and whose genetic material met their needs. Someone made a selection with transplants and there were always criteria for those decisions.

Would the person survive the operation, was the condition likely to return? Whose lives would be affected if they didn't get the organs: their children, their work? Had their lifestyle choices contributed to them having the condition? And, of course, eventually, when healthcare had to be paid for, could they afford the medical interventions on offer?'

'All I am doing is arguing that the world then could extend a level of compassion to the needy and a response to people's wants that is simply not possible for us. That may not appear compassionate, but it is reality. Our duty now is to manage and sustain the Community's population, not allow our emotions, personal attachments and selfish wants as individuals to rule us.'

Lucy was not convinced. 'This just makes us sound like machines.'

Jude nodded slowly. 'That is not the intention. We are much more than that. We are capable of great vision, extraordinary acts of self denial and sacrifice. We can use our brains and intuition, our sense of justice about right and wrong and make hard choices. Over time I have come to think that any offering up of a life will be viewed not as a sacrifice that individuals are making, but rather a gift that they are choosing to give to the Community as a whole.'

'That's pathetic!' Lucy was almost bursting with frustration. 'I don't want to hear any more! A gift's something you give because you want to show you care for someone. This just feels like...' she struggled for the word '...guilt. It's survival of the fittest. Being made to do something terrible that you don't want to do because if you don't then people will think you're selfish.'

Jude spoke, slowly and quietly, but firmly.

'Lucy, I am very mindful of the challenge. But you must understand. Our very existence hangs by a thread. Genetically our longer term existence depends on diversity, but in the short term we can't afford to invest resources in people that cannot work or contribute positively. Eventually, if all goes well, we will outgrow the useful space the island can offer. We could establish a second settlement on the mainland where we can start to farm in a bigger area. But that settlement must also focus on the ultimate goal, the 'big picture', saving the species. We cannot allow arguments about an individual's right to life or choice of partner to take precedence over our collective responsibilities to sustain the Community.'

Lucy shifted uncomfortably.

'Believe me, Lucy, I wish we were not in this situation. But, through no fault of our own, we are. I am Chief Steward. I have had to apply logic rather than sentiment to this. But I can't do this alone. I need help to save the Community, to explain, justify and cement the way of living, and the way of dying, that I am proposing so it becomes part of the very fabric and culture of the Community. I believe if we all understand better that we are, at least in part, victims of previous indecision, not aggressors, we will embrace Duty Calls as all good citizens should.'

Lucy remained unconvinced. 'Why are you telling me all this?'

'A good question.' Jude's face softened and his tone became almost tender. 'It is because I see something very special in you, Lucy. I see a wisdom that is beyond your years, a determination and tenacity. Yes, you can be hot tempered at times, and passionate, but that is not necessarily a bad thing, if it can be directed. Young people listen to you and the future lies in their hands. I have chosen you for this task because I have high hopes for you, my dear.'

Jude paused, and placing his hand gently on her head, spoke very clearly, his eyes burning into hers, his words intense with meaning. 'You would be doing this work, not for me, but for those you love: for Seb, for Anna, for your mother. You would be doing it for those that are alive now and for all those to come.'

Lucy sat back in her chair, her body rigid and mouth dry. She wanted to flinch and every part of her skin tingled at Jude's touch. She wasn't convinced, but Jude was persuasive and a clever orator. And she could not help it, for an instant she felt something else. Special. The Chief Steward was choosing her to do something he believed would help everyone she cared for in the here and now, but also leave a legacy for the future.

She rested her elbows on the table, cradling her head and closing her eyes. By now the sunshine had fully permeated through the windows and was illuminating the room, though even at its brightest it was still not possible to see fully into the darkest corners. Lucy realised that she was almost faint with hunger.

'I need to eat, Jude,' she whispered. 'It's a while since breakfast.'

'Of course, we must always remember to feed the body as well as the mind and soul. I have prepared some soup which I hope will refresh you.' He surveyed her keenly. 'Perhaps you would like to take some air while I warm it for us? It should not take me too long.'

Lucy opened the door and emerged thankfully out into the warm autumn sunshine. Not for the first time she longed for Anna. It was at times like these that she most missed her Mum. For a moment she had to screw up her eyes. Lela stood immediately, and clinging closely to her heels followed her to the spit of land that looked over towards the glistening waters of the sea stretching away into the distance. She luxuriated in the peacefulness and sense of space and history that always took hold of her when she was near the coast, allowing the rhythmic sound of the timeless ebb and flow of the waves to calm her.

After a few minutes she slowly made her way back to the cottage. She found Jude standing in the doorway, looking out across the square, nodding and responding to greetings from various villagers going purposefully about their daily chores. Was it her imagination or did they each appear to stride more energetically as they passed him?

'Ah, Lucy, come in. Lunch is ready for you.' Seeing Lela at her heels, Jude indicated a bowl of fresh water he had placed at the doorstep and some scraps of meat and vegetables that the dog sniffed at, wolfing down appreciatively.

Inside, Lucy was greeted by two steaming bowls of hot broth and some fresh bread. Jude had lit a small fire in the grate and there was a blackened pot standing over it, steaming slightly. They ate in silence. The soup was warming and surprisingly tasty, almost as good as Anna's, thick with vegetables and a stock that was resonant with fresh herbs. Mopping up the dregs with the bread Lucy sighed appreciatively. She had needed that.

Collecting the bowls, Jude took them behind a heavy curtain that sectioned off the washing and cooking area from the room. Returning he smiled down on her.

'I like to take a short time for rest and contemplation after my meals, Lucy. You are welcome to stay or perhaps you would prefer to enjoy the fresh air. This afternoon I want to show you the place where, should you agree, you would undertake the Duty Calls task I have in mind for you.'

Lucy suspected that Jude's reflection would take the form of prayer and contemplation in front of the cross that hung behind him. She supposed that believing there was a purpose and some kind of force for good that was looking out for them all, and an afterlife to look forward to, brought its own solace. But she had always struggled with acceptance of a higher Authority and it was difficult to believe in a benevolent force in a world where it felt that so many had needlessly died.

She decided to take a stroll with Lela around the village streets. Everyone must be busy either indoors or in the fields, because she saw no one. The gardens were full of colour and filled to overflowing with rows of fruit and vegetables. The trees that were dotted around the landscape were all wearing their autumnal colours, russet browns and oranges, the light breeze blowing the leaves every so often in a flurry so they whirled and danced to the ground.

Lucy kicked through where they had blown into damp and glistening piles, loving the familiar crunching sound of her boots as they slid through them, transporting her, momentarily, back to her childhood walks with her Mum. Kicking through leaves had always been a way of marking and ticking off another year together. Some things always stay the same, she thought. It's just that maybe no one really knows how they will end.

The Castle

She returned to the cottage and, as she approached, Jude was emerging. He indicated the path towards the Castle at the end of the spit of land that stretched out into the sea. 'We'll walk and talk,' he said. 'It will be pleasant on this wonderful afternoon and good for me to exercise my old bones.' Jude set a slow pace, so she was easily able to fall into step beside him and Lela trotted along quite happily, enjoying this unexpected excursion.

The ancient Castle loomed up in front of them, a sombre ruin, its weathered grey brown walls giving it a sense of desolation that stirred old memories of a tumultuous past. It stood cradled on a medieval hillock, a cobbled footpath winding its way from the base to the Castle gate. Nodding towards the approaching edifice Jude continued. 'I understand the need to see our loved ones making their transition from life to death in a way that acknowledges the nobility of their sacrifice. My vision is to create a place for Duty Calls to be enacted and celebrated, here in the courtyard of the old Castle.'

'You mean this is where people would come to die?'

'I would hope that it will be associated not just with dying, sacrifice and giving, but also with receiving. I want it to be the Community's place of transition. And somewhere for each of us one day to experience a final ceremony, genuine compassion and the expression of real appreciation from the whole Community of the lives we have lived and the deaths we have chosen.'

Kittiwakes whirled in the sky above them, heading out to sea. Lucy could hear the sound of lapwings calling to each other behind her. There was such contrast between the freedom of life in the Nature that was all around her and the description of this managed and controlled way of living life and deciding death that Jude was proposing.

Eventually they reached the Castle gate and passed through into an inner courtyard. The first thing her eyes fell upon was a brass plaque screwed to a wall and tucked out of the way of the wind and elements. It was covered in a script she did not recognise.

'What's this?' she asked, peering at the spidery runes. 'I've never seen anything like it.'

Jude came over and stood looking at the text. 'This part of the Castle was once used as a hospital wing for wounded soldiers. The plaque shows something called the Hippocratic Oath. The words would have been familiar to your mother. It has been here for years. It describes the foundations on which all physicians in the past based their ethical behaviour. Here,' and he ran his finger over the writing, 'it says *"And I will use treatments for the benefit of the ill in accordance with my ability and my judgment, but from what is to their harm and injustice I will keep them."*

'Our forefathers took this to mean that doctors would always act in the best interests of their patients. When unjust circumstances arose, say if a certain life saving drug or resource was not available, they would strive to correct the injustice arising from that scarcity and do everything they could to prevent that absence from harming their patients. You would agree with that I'm sure?'

'Course. They'd have expected to be able to trust a doctor to give them what they needed to get better or show them how not to get ill.'

'It says here,' and Jude again ran his finger across the runes: *"And I will not give a drug that is deadly to anyone if asked, nor will I suggest the way to such a counsel."*

'I know that what I am suggesting in Duty Calls appears to fly in the face of this promise. But many started to believe that this passage alluded to the common practice at the time this Oath was first devised of using doctors as skilled political assassins. Of course, they would have wanted doctors to swear not to use their knowledge and skills to assassinate.'

Jude looked hard at her. 'The word '*euthanasia*' means '*easeful death.*' That describes something with a sense that is very different from assassination. Think of it, Lucy, an '*easeful death*'. Which of us would not want that for our loved ones?'

'I'd rather choose an easeful life,' spluttered Lucy, shaking her head. 'It's all we can do to look after ourselves now. Why would we put time into ceremonies for the dying? It doesn't make any sense!'

'You're right, we would be investing resources, our time and energy, into the process. But by honouring those who submit to Duty Calls as heroes we would be creating the culture we need, helping the Community to play for the far bigger prize, the saving of the species.'

They passed through into a wide, open natural amphitheatre protected from the wind by the high stone walls but with a clear view up into the sky.

'This is where I envisage holding ceremonies of remembrance for those that have taken the Duty Calls pathway.'

Making his way to the centre Jude stopped and swept his arms around an area a few metres across.

'And here we would erect a memorial with the names of all those that we want to honour for doing their duty. We could celebrate their sacrifice each year on New Year's Eve. And the first celebration would be in three months time to mark and coincide with the start of the new century. Your mother would be one of the first to be remembered.'

Lucy muttered. 'You've got it all worked out.'

'Planning is vital. My father used to say that planning was a powerful tool. It makes projects sustainable, delivers many benefits to a Community including certainty and confidence, rights and protection for our environment, heritage and biodiversity. For the sake of our children and grandchildren, planning must be seen as a force for good. Do you see Lucy, how with hindsight his words now seem so wise, so prophetic? The message is simple: good planning makes better, safer communities. We all might want our Community to place social justice, equality and resources at the heart of planning decisions. Just imagine the world we would be living in now if his words had been listened to and acted upon more rigorously.'

'I believe in an afterlife, as you know Lucy. So death, essentially, holds no fear for me. But that's not the point. The point is that we have a duty to fulfil our function in the here and now. And I believe our key function is to steward whatever resources we have responsibly, including ourselves.'

Lucy was really starting to struggle. This was the argument her Mum had swallowed when she had given up her own life so as not to be a burden to others.

'Why should we be expected to make these sorts of horrible decisions? It's not natural that we should do this to people we love.'

'My vision is that Duty Calls is a way of showing love. This would be somewhere each of us in the Community comes for a regular check up throughout our lives. I envisage each visit resulting in either a continuation of an individual's existing work, or a chance to be reassigned something more suited to that person's skills and capabilities as those change over time. It would not just be a place of endings; it would also be a place of new beginnings.'

With a last glance around, Jude led Lucy out of the Castle. Settling himself on an old stone slab he gestured for her to join him. They sat for few moments in silence, taking in everything that they could see. The Castle loomed behind them, a series of towers and archways, its rough hewn stone columns reaching like fingers into the clear blue sky.

Eventually Jude broke the silence. 'This is a site of peace and reflection for me. The view out to sea hasn't changed since the dawn of time. It gives me such a different perspective on the village. Look Lucy.' He raised his right hand and made a fist, with only his thumb pointing to the sky. 'Close one eye and look back. From here you can block out the entire village. Our Community may be the whole world to us, but when we look at it from this perspective, you can see how little we are in it all. We are, even all of us together, just a tiny heartbeat in history.'

Eventually Jude sighed and helped Lucy to her feet. Holding her hands in his, he stood looking at her for a moment, his face impassive. Unable to stop herself, Lucy blushed and looked down. He let her go.

'Come. It is time for me to show you the part in the Duty Calls Project that I have in mind for you.'

The pair began to return along the well trodden path. Jude paused and, looking pensive for a moment he glanced back at the Castle. 'So many, many people have travelled this way,' he mused. 'I would like to think that we can help many more to do the same.'

Lucy glanced across at Jude as they walked together. His face in profile was much sharper and his features more angular than when seen from the front. The aquiline nose and slightly hooded eyes were more obvious from this angle. In spite of the warm sunshine she felt suddenly cold.

'So, what is this *'opportunity'* then? Is it hard?'

Jude stopped, stood still and turned to stare out into the sea. When he spoke it was no longer as an elder or a superior. Turning to Lucy, he grasped her wrists and fixed her with his steady gaze. Now he spoke in the tones of a confidante.

'Lucy, this will be a glorious work. In a few weeks we will have reached the end of this century and the start of the next. I want us to have a Duty Calls event in the Castle that will bring together the whole Community, welcome in the new century and launch the Project. At the heart of this event will be a story to be presented to everyone that will explain and justify why we have to make these choices. It is a story that I would like you to tell.'

Jude let go of her wrists and stood watching her closely, appearing to take in every detail of her both inside and out.

'Only you can do this, Lucy. None of the others, not Anna, not Seb, no one else. You are the one I have chosen. You alone will shed a light on the past and shine a beacon into the future. You will leave a story that will be both a lesson to us now and a legacy for all those that follow.'

Lucy listened, her mind suffused with a whole mixture of emotions. It was really hard to process everything that Jude had shared with her. But for the first time in her life she felt something with absolute certainty. She longed to be remembered. She wanted to be special. But even more than that, she believed she had to do something. Because if what Jude said came to pass, it was only a matter of time until one day it would be the turn of someone else she loved to be a candidate for Duty Calls.

The Time Capsule

By now their footsteps had taken them almost into the village. Instead of going back to his cottage, Jude turned down a narrow lane leading to the island's ancient church. It nestled where it had stood for generations on a small plot, a churchyard on three sides, a simple spire that pointed heavenwards, the whole building conveying an air of timelessness and peaceful tranquillity. Pushing open the heavy wooden door they passed into the cool interior. Crossing the aisle Jude led the way to a small entrance, heavily carved and, using a large blackened metal key from his pocket, he turned the lock.

The door opened to reveal a short staircase down into a crypt. Reaching inside and feeling along a ridge on the wall Jude picked up a piece of paper and a sharp flint that lay on a shelf of rock. Striking this expertly he created a few sparks, one of which caught the paper which instantly flared. He used it as a taper to light a candle which he fixed into an ancient holder.

Shadows instantly danced across the ceiling and the wall ahead. Leading the way, Jude stepped carefully down into a tiny room containing an old wooden table, a heavy armchair with a high back and a cushion of embroidered tapestry. On the table was something flat and box shaped, covered in a faded red velvet cloth.

Setting the candlestick holder on the table Jude motioned Lucy to the chair. Once seated, he moved behind the table and stood motionless, each of his hands tucked into the opposite sleeve of his robe, the light illuminating his face eerily from below.

'Lucy, what I am about to show you now must remain our secret. It has existed since my father's time and it was he who told me about it. He gave me the key to this room before he died and made me promise that one day, when the time was right, I would make use of it in the best way I could. I believe we have reached that day.'

With a swift movement Jude pulled the cloth from the object and folding it neatly placed it on the end of the table. Lucy gasped. What was in front of her was something that belonged to a time long gone, something that she remembered from articles she had read about her grandparents' childhoods, but had only ever seen in pictures.

It lay on the table, a silver grey, thin rectangular case, not much bigger than a large book. Jude slid a button at the front and lifted the lid. In spite of herself Lucy felt awed. How had this machine survived? She reached forward and very gently ran her fingers over the keys, hardly daring to breathe. In the midst of her world of wood and earth and clay it was a piece of magic, like a mysterious comet that had returned to remind her of a world that had gone before.

'A laptop! I don't believe it. How ever did this get here?'

Jude became animated, clearly delighted by her reaction. 'This is a treasure, hidden many years ago. It is not like the laptops my father knew as a child. It does not, as far as I am aware, connect with the outside world. Although...' moving the candle to the floor to illuminate the area under the desk '...as you can see there is a tangle of wires running into the wall.' Jude hesitated momentarily. 'Those are not your concern. What is important, however, is that it can play this.'

Reaching into a pocket in his robe, Jude drew out a small blue and silver object, just a few centimetres in length and held it carefully between his thumb and forefinger.

'Have you ever seen one of these Lucy? It's a memory stick, a data storage key. It's almost fifty years old. It was made around 2050. We can plug this into the laptop here,' he indicated a notched area on one side of the machine 'and it will download all the information about our history that my father and his associates collected and saved from the past. You will be amazed how much can be stored on so small an object.'

He held the tiny rectangle in front of him and it glistened in the candlelight. 'This memory stick is a key, Lucy, a Time Capsule. From time to time as Chief Steward I have come here and studied it. No one else has seen the items stored here for almost fifty years. Once plugged in you unlock it by entering a password and then the contents are displayed on the screen.'

Lucy could barely take in what she was hearing. This was not what she had been expecting at all. 'I had no idea! Where did it come from? How on earth was it made? Where does it get its energy from?'

'It doesn't need much energy to work. It's powered by a solar panel high up on the church tower. My father was part of a team of eco warriors, educationalists, computer experts that had worked on developing the Time Capsule's archive as a Project. They started working in 2030 and continued to store materials till 2050. For reasons that will become clear, if you take on the assignment, they called the Project the *20/20 Vision*. Essentially they wanted to create something that was part archive, part flare. A warning, a means to tell a story but also educate those that they hoped would one day find it and learn from the mistakes of the past.'

Indicating a wooden stool for Lucy, Jude settled into the chair at the table and continued. Lucy's pulse was racing, her hands moist. She could not drag her eyes away from the machine.

'My father was Isaac Goodman. He worked very closely on this Project with my uncle, Nick Grigori. They met as students at university around 2015. The two families, the Goodmans and the Grigoris were related through marriage.

'My father and Nick were very different characters, but those differences were kept quite hidden. I only knew of them through the conversations I overheard between them as I grew up. Nick Grigori was an idealist, much as you are I think Lucy, my father more of a realist. I believe I am more like him.'

'My uncle Nick had a child, a daughter. She was my cousin. As young children we were very close, much like you and Seb are. But as we grew up and the differences between our two families became more pronounced we spent less time together and drifted apart. I suspect both sets of parents developed different expectations and that was reflected in the way they chose to bring us up.'

'What was her name?' asked Lucy.

Jude smiled sarcastically. 'Something that was rather typical of the Grigori family I fear. They called her *Hope*.'

Lucy's eyes were drawn back to the laptop and Jude stroked it, barely able to conceal his excitement. 'I see you are impressed by the machine. Do you also recall the powers it had from things your grandparents told you? Computers were as much a part of their lives as farm tools are for us today. And this one, once the key is entered, is a portal to the past. If you use it to access the data stored on this small but incredibly powerful device you can see events that have been hidden, frozen in time.'

'It is a means of accessing a whole range of material stored in ways that even I can barely remember: Google, Facebook, Messenger, You Tube, newsreels from the 21st century. These were all methods of communicating and sharing events, stories, information. My father and Nick led the Project with a small group of other far sighted people who were driven by their desire to leave the only legacy that they believed mattered. Think of it as a reference library, Lucy, a highly sophisticated message in a bottle. You will find a series of stories about how people then dealt with highly problematic global events. Those actions have led to the way of life we have today.'

Lucy could hardly breathe. Was this really a way to see images that had been covered up for more than 50 years?

Jude continued. 'Computer technology was still available in parts of the world right up until the middle of this century. Its power to communicate was awesome. You will have heard your grandparents talking about the World Wide Web?'

Lucy nodded. 'Yeah, it sounded incredible. Kind of scary, but exciting at the same time.'

'You weren't born till 2082, so you grew up never experiencing computers. I did however. They were around all through my childhood so I can help you to get started. I will steer you to the most relevant material. Of course it will take you a little time to familiarise yourself with the techniques for working through the information, but the way the Time Capsule has been constructed allows for this. They expected and built in a means to show techniques to access and use the information, ways that will enable you to search through it, so you can tell the story of the past and thus set the context for the future.'

'I must impress upon you though Lucy that I'd need you to move quite quickly through the material, select the key facts and produce the story I would want you to share. You would have only seven weeks to complete the assignment if we are to have everything ready in time for the end of the year. You would come here once a week to work. I'd have liked to have given you longer but the Community simply cannot spare you from your other duties.'

Lucy shrugged her shoulders. 'That wouldn't bother me.'

Jude nodded. 'There will be tensions that you will find in creating a story that will need to be 'good enough' when you are

65

likely to want to explore in greater depth. To help you therefore I have prepared a list of questions to get you started. I would need you to look over those tonight so you can start tomorrow.'

'And you must not breathe a word of what you find out to Anna or Seb. That would spoil the surprise of New Year. We will simply tell them you are working for me.'

This was an awesome secret. However Lucy knew immediately that, whatever she promised Jude, there was no way she could keep this from Anna and Seb. Jude was very much mistaken if he really believed she would ever do that. But she could hardly breathe with excitement. In spite of her initial reservations, she was overwhelmed with curiosity, pride at being chosen and desire to see into the past. Where was the harm in learning from that? As far as she could tell, while she might hate the idea of Duty Calls herself, Jude's stewardship intentions were, from his perspective at least, wholly benevolent.

He spent the next hour pointing out various features on the laptop so she could operate it. It seemed simple enough. Eventually he held up the heavy metal door key and a small notebook. A pencil was tied by a string to its spine.

'Here is the key to the room and a book for you to make notes. If you agree to take on the task, you will return the key to me each day so you can report back on your progress. If I am called away on other business I will leave it for you under the large blue stone next to the doorpost at my front gate. The memory stick you will leave here. There is no time to lose. I want you to begin in earnest tomorrow.'

With great care Jude held out his hand so Lucy could take the tiny storage device, if she chose to do so.

'Well Lucy, what do you think? You and the other young people are the future of our Community, not me. One day you will need to take on the responsibilities for that future and of that leadership between you. Are you ready to start on that journey?'

She was tempted. What harm could it do? If she learned anything about the past that could help Anna and Seb she might even do some good. Lucy took the memory stick from his hand and wrapped her fingers firmly round it.

'I am.'

Jude gave her a gracious and kindly smile. 'Bless you for that my child. I have every confidence in you. One last thing though, Lucy. I must tell you the password to access the archive, which of course you must take with you to your grave. It is the title of my Uncle Nick's favourite film. A classic of its time you might say and one in fact that he used to watch with Hope and me when we were children.'

Jude paused dramatically and then, although there was no one else there, he wrapped an arm around Lucy's shoulders and drew her face to his. She could smell his breath stale on her cheek as he whispered into her ear.

'The password is *Avatar*.'

On the first day

Opening her eyes, Lucy felt even before she was fully conscious that something had changed. For a few moments her thoughts rolled round her mind like tumbleweed. Then she woke up fully and remembered instantly why this morning was different.

The Time Capsule!

She did not exactly leap out of bed, but she certainly rose with a greater sense of focus and determination than she had felt for some time. Finally she had something to get her teeth into, something to give purpose to her existence. Of course, there were always things to do: food to grow, repairs to make, clothes to wash. But those were not the activities that gave meaning to life. All they did were to allow her to exist. Now everything was different. Her destiny was tied up inextricably with what she would find when she accessed that data.

As she went to the door she picked one of the seven smooth pebbles she had chosen from the shoreline on her way home and dropped it into the blue clay bowl on her window ledge. 'Day One' she said out loud and, with Lela as always trotting faithfully at her heels, she stepped out into the morning.

The previous night she and Seb had walked the dog along the shoreline before turning in for the night. She had tried to keep the conversation on Anna, wondering whether she would bring any news back from her trip to the lighthouse. He had wanted to know everything about her time with Jude of course.

'So what did he want, the old creep?' asked Seb as they skimmed pebbles out into the water. Lucy hesitated, mindful of her promise to keep this laptop secret.

'I've been given a job to do, for the New Year celebrations,' she mumbled.

'What kind of a job?'

'I've got to help with the entertainment.'

'Why'd he choose you? Can't see you singing for your supper,' Seb teased. 'It's got to be something more than that.'

'I don't know why I got chosen. I'm going to be telling a story, sort of our Community's history up till now, how we came to exist.'

'How you going to do that?' asked Seb. 'Most people who know that stuff are long dead.'

She tried to stop him asking questions. 'Jude's got some old documents I can look through. All pretty boring really.'

Seb was not stupid. He guessed from the way she tried to change the subject that there was more to this than Lucy was willing to share. But he was not going to pressurise her to tell him. He suspected she would never be able to keep anything a secret from him for very long. He walked her back home, both of them lost in their thoughts. When they reached their yard he gave her a swift hug as usual and they parted to settle down for the night in their separate dwellings.

In the morning, as Lucy set off, Anna's cottage with Seb inside was in darkness and there was an empty space where yesterday the horse and cart had stood ready for the regular trip to the lighthouse to check for refugees. Those trips had become less frequent as numbers had steadily decreased and lacked any of the optimism they had generated in the past. It was inevitable that one day they would simply not be deemed worth the effort and cease. *'Bet that day's not far away,'* Lucy thought to herself.

Hurrying through the village, she knocked at Jude's door. There was no answer, so she collected the key from under the stone at the entrance and made her way directly to the church. She half ran, half skipped along. Today was going to be the start of a journey. She was going to see the destruction of one way of life and the evolution of another. She would gain perspectives on that story which she had never had before. Perhaps, and here she suddenly stopped in her tracks as the thought brought her up short, these perspectives would throw a different light for her on Duty Calls?

Lucy had wondered about Jude's decision in choosing her and could not help feeling a slight twinge at being selected. Was this pride? Her heart was beating faster, excited by the prospect of what lay ahead and of the responsibility and trust that the Chief Steward had placed in her. She sensed that the story she would pull together had the potential to make a real difference.

Reaching the church, Lucy slipped in, crossed directly to the door that led to the crypt, opened it with the heavy key and lit one of the candles Jude had left inside. Closing the door behind her and,

70

hesitating for a moment, she turned the key and locked herself in. It felt strange. It had never been necessary to lock anything in the Community and she could not remember the last time she had even turned a key. But intuitively, without quite being able to put her finger on why, she wanted to make sure she could not be watched.

Making her way down the steps, Lucy dropped her bag to the floor and settled herself into the chair. Lela lay down at her feet. Taking a deep breath she leaned forward, removed the cloth from the laptop and pushed the 'On' button. There was a moment's hesitation and then a low whirring sound as the machine sprang into life. Removing a small bundle of cloth from her pocket she carefully unwrapped the memory stick and took it from the box she had put it in the night before. She ran her fingers around each side of the machine and felt a gap in the surface towards the front on the right. Holding both ends of the device she gave a slight tug and a cap slid off, revealing a tiny metal prong. It exactly fitted into the gap.

A message appeared on screen asking for the password. Slowly flexing her fingers in preparation she carefully typed the letters Jude had given her: AVATAR. The screen went initially blank and then a number of pictures Jude had explained were called icons appeared and then a cursor. She was on her way.

Barely thinking, Lucy started to operate the mouse pad as Jude had described she should and move the cursor. Hovering over the icon for the *20/20 Vision* folder that appeared she touched the mouse quickly with her index finger and heard a faint click. Instantly the folder opened. Within seconds the screen was showing a front page with a patchwork of images: oceans and rain forests, close ups of individuals and a family group. The centre point was a moving picture of a gently opening door. The symbolism was obvious. The programme was inviting her to enter. Mindful of Jude's instructions about the need to be shown how to use the material, Lucy held her breath and dived in.

Almost immediately the head and shoulders of a man appeared on the screen. He was about Anna's age, with intelligent eyes, thick tousled hair greying at the temples, a lived in face that fell easily into its well worn laughter lines and a warm smile. Next to him sat a second man who she identified immediately as almost certainly Jude's father. The family resemblance was unmistakeable. The first man began to speak.

'Hello. My name is Nick Grigori. Welcome to the 20/20 Vision project. The date is 2050 and I am one of the Project's coordinators.

'You have accessed a programme of archived data that is the culmination of almost twenty years of work carried out by a small team of volunteers. We started in 2030 and have completed it just as the World Wide Web is becoming inaccessible. We are a team of men and women from a range of backgrounds: environmentalists, biologists, physicists, chemists, geologists, medics, web designers, spiritual leaders, eco warriors.' He nodded to the man next to him. 'Central to the team is my close friend and brother-in-law, Isaac Goodman.'

Lucy smiled to herself. She had been right.

Isaac took up the narrative. *'We have no idea who or indeed if anyone will remain alive to access this data, but we are driven by a real sense that time is running out for the way of life we have known and that much of what is happening to our planet today is irreversible. This Project, we feel, is a way to have our learning preserved and our voices one day heard. We feel we have no choice but to try. It is our duty.'*

Nick continued the address. *'The 20/20 Vision team believes that 'telling' or 'scaring' people typically doesn't work in bringing about changes in behaviour. We want anyone that accesses the stories contained in this data store to think, discuss and make their own truth from the events that we have researched and preserved here. We believe that is the best way to change how you in turn choose to act.'*

'The data is stored in such a way that you should be able to find your own path through it. There is a timeline that you can click on' and here a screen shot of a calendar appeared *'so you could go to a date that is significant for you, for example a birthday, and find out what was going on then. Or you can search by a keyword or a question. Or you can simply click on a file, open it, sit back and watch the stories unfold rather as you might watch a film.'*

As Nick explained the process Isaac demonstrated what to do on the screen. Lucy was able to copy him and quickly picked up the way to use the mouse to move the cursor across the screen, click on the various icons and access the search facility. It was overwhelming to her how much data could be contained within such a tiny device.

73

There was no chance she could keep this a secret. She could not wait till the evening to be able to talk to Anna and Seb about it all.

'I wonder if Gramps and Grandma had one of these at home?' she thought. The idea that ordinary people could have something so magical and powerful as a laptop in their own house made her breathless. Not for the first time she felt herself raging inside at the sense of loss and waste of resources and the injustice of all she and Seb had missed out on as a consequence.

Isaac continued the tutorial.

'You can use the search facility to explore old newsreels and articles relating to changes in the biological, political, medical, geographical, natural environments that were happening from the early part of the twentieth century. For example, you could start with a question like 'What was global warming?' and the programme would select from the data you have downloaded and give you information to help you find out more.'

'There is no 'right' or 'wrong' way to do your search. Different people will start with different questions depending on your areas of interest and take different paths through the information. The 20/20 Vision team expect that anyone accessing this data will be doing so in a world that has changed out of all recognition from the one Nick and I know. We want you to draw your own conclusions about why those changes have taken place. We want this Project to be a lens to magnify the lessons from the past, but also a means to explore and get right the planning for any Community that survives in the future.'

'It is our belief that by the time anyone sees this it will probably be impossible to turn the clock back. We are putting our trust in the human capacity to learn and adapt to survive. Perhaps we are naive, but in spite of the evidence of the lack of foresight that has created the situation we find ourselves in, we still have faith and hope.'

At this point Nick took over.

'I fully expect that by the time this data store is accessed I will be long dead and probably so will everyone I know. But as a parent, I needed to do this for anyone, anyone at all, who might still be alive long after I'm gone.'

He leaned forward and stared intently into the camera. Lucy felt he was looking directly at her. 'We all have choices. Whoever you are you have a huge responsibility to see this data and use its messages to inform those choices. I would say one last thing to you. I beg you, don't just look. See.'

The images of the two men faded and Lucy was left once again with the front page and a set of icons. She sat back in the chair, looking steadily at the screen, overwhelmed. So this was it. It was far more extraordinary than she could ever have imagined. Nothing Jude had said had really prepared her. This was mind blowing.

She spent the next couple of hours simply familiarising herself with how the laptop and the programme worked. Eventually Lucy realised she had gone as far as she could for one day. She was exhausted. The candle had almost burnt down and was starting to splutter a last gasp. With a sigh she logged out, removing the memory stick. She again wrapped it carefully and put it securely in the wooden box she had brought with her and placed it on the table. With a final glance round the room, she draped the cloth over the laptop, unlocked the door, securing it behind her and made her way out of the church and back through the village, Lela at her heels.

At Jude's cottage she knocked and almost immediately the door was opened. Glancing up and down the street, he drew her quickly inside, took the crypt key from her and indicated a seat by the table. The pair sat together in silence for a moment while Lucy gathered her thoughts which were spinning around her head. Jude was leaning forward, his expression one of eager anticipation.

'Well, Lucy. You look tired.'

Without lifting her eyes, she nodded. 'It's been a long day.'

'I must know how you got on. I will make you some tea.'

Disappearing into the kitchen area, Jude returned a few moments later with a steaming mug. 'I had just made this, I suspected you would be back soon,' he said handing it to her.

Sipping the tea appreciatively, Lucy began to describe what she had done, what she had understood about the way the data was organised, what her initial ideas were for searching for the information that would make the best story. In spite of her tiredness, the words tumbled from her in a breathless stream.

'Your father and Nick Grigori must have been extraordinary people,' she said eventually. 'They had incredible commitment. They put so much time and energy into developing this Project.'

Jude looked quizzical. 'That's an interesting perspective. I'm afraid I'm less generous in my assessment.'

'Really, why?'

'They had years to do something about what was happening to our planet and did nothing but talk. I however have a plan and want to put Duty Calls into action at the first opportunity we have in order to save us all.'

' Isaac was my father. I have never been a parent. But I would like to think that if I was I would do everything in my power to make the world a safe place in the here and now for my child and the children of others to grow up and survive. I have no doubt the *20/20 Vision* team came to the Project with good intentions. But, given everything that has happened since, they do appear to have been somewhat passive and naive, to say the very least. I'm afraid I see them as a bunch of rather ineffectual academics, who said they cared, but really made very little difference and were quickly forgotten. I intend to be very different.'

Lucy finished her tea and made her way home, tired and reflective. As she walked up the lane she saw the horse and cart outside her cottage and noted that Anna was back from her overnight trip to the lighthouse. So much had happened since she had left the day before. Her mind went back to the bitter disappointment they had felt at the same time the year previously, a disappointment that had been repeated many times since, and she did not even think to knock and ask if there was any better news today. Instead she opened the door into her cottage, selected a handful of vegetables from her pantry and began to prepare supper for them all. As she did so she suddenly froze. How strange that Jude had not said anything.

It was her 17th birthday.

On the second day

A whole week had passed in chores and harvesting. This was a time of preparation for winter. Seb had joined a group of other young men who had been set the task of finding enough wood to see them through. He had returned each night, filthy and covered in sweat, flopping onto the old sofa and closing his eyes.

'Don't know how long I can keep this up for,' he would mutter.

Lucy woke on Monday, went through her normal routines and, dropping the latch to her cottage behind her and with an eager anticipation made her way down to the church, again collecting the key on her way. There was no sign of Jude.

In just seven days the evidence that autumn was advancing was everywhere. Trees were still leaf bearing, but there were far more piling up into corners and along ridges and kerbs. They lay waiting to be swept up and moved into the various mulching hillocks that were starting to appear dotted around the gardens and landscape.

As she entered the churchyard her eyes rested on the corner where the unmarked grave she, Anna and Seb had dug only a year before lay hidden. The wild flowers they had scattered there were long dead. She stopped and, glancing round, quickly gathered some more to replace them and then turned towards the church. The memory of what had happened to Sam made her even more determined to make the most of the opportunity she had been given.

Slipping inside, Lucy walked directly to the crypt door. Using the candle she had brought with her to guide her she moved quickly to the desk and settled almost immediately to the task in hand. She unfolded the paper with the questions Jude had given her that she had been thinking about in the intervening week and smoothed it flat so she could read the first one.

'What was known of global warming in 2020?'

Turning on the laptop Lucy skipped past the tutorial given by Nick and Isaac and made her way to the search facility where she could type her question into a box. Her fingers moved slowly over the keys, it would take her a while to get up to speed. But she managed, and once she had checked that she had asked what she wanted her finger hovered momentarily and then pressed the Enter key.

For the next two hours Lucy barely broke her concentration for more than a few moments. She learnt to scroll through the various articles, video clips and other material that she could highlight from the list that appeared and she could choose from. Everything she read threw up more questions and then she would start to dig deeper by refining her search, typing in more specific questions and allowing the programme to sift out the most relevant material from its archive. All she uncovered amazed her. She could barely contain her sense of disbelief and could not wait to talk to Anna and Seb.

Over supper with them that night Lucy tried to explain what it had been like. As Seb had suspected she had not been able to keep the details a secret and had already regaled them with everything Jude had shown her during her first encounter with the laptop, swearing them both to a secrecy she had complete trust that they would maintain. They were, if anything, even more amazed and disbelieving than she had been. They could hardly wait to hear how she had got on during her second visit.

'There was just so much, I couldn't cope,' Lucy sighed, flopping in an exhausted heap into the comfort of the armchair next to the fire and watching Anna stirring the stew. 'I just tried to sort out a timeline for all the stuff that had happened.'

What kind of stuff?' asked Seb.

'Hurricanes, tsunamis, droughts, sea levels going up, ice caps melting, changes in water quality. There was so much happening to the climate back then, people just seemed to get used to it. Or maybe some of them just didn't feel they could do anything.'

'But the more I went on, you could see how all these bad things happening together left us all, the whole world, really vulnerable. It was a like a set of dominoes going down. One thing led to another and nothing could stop it.'

Anna started to dish the rabbit and vegetable stew into bowls and the three sat down at the worn farmhouse table.

'Here you go, eat,' said Anna. 'You must be starving.'

There was a moment of appreciative silence. After a few mouthfuls Seb spoke up.

'Come on Lucy, I want to know everything.'

'Hold on, Seb,' said Anna. 'She's got to eat. It sounds like the story is going to be that the earth and all of us on it are connected. That's not exactly a surprise.' The three of them focused on their food for a few more minutes, but Seb could not contain himself.

'Did everything just happen really fast then?'

'Yes,' mumbled Lucy through a mouthful of stew. 'And it wasn't like people couldn't see it coming. They did. And they had loads of ways of telling each other about it. They had television and films and the internet and they had conferences and talked loads and tried to agree what they should do. Honestly, I couldn't believe how much they talked!'

'So why the hell didn't they *do* something?' cried Seb. 'I mean, we talk about stuff here all the time but when we know something's wrong we act.'

Lucy shook her head trying to get an answer. 'I know, like we saved the harvest last year, because we had to.'

Seb was furious. 'Exactly, we worked all night on it. No one complained.'

'Jude says it's because in the Community we work as one family,' Lucy mused. 'It's because there's so few of us we all look out for each other because we know we all need each other. We know none of us can do stuff on our own. It wasn't like that in the olden days. Some people just seemed focused on their own little bit. They sort of missed the big picture.'

'Sounds pretty selfish to me,' muttered Seb, mopping up the last of his stew.

'Yeah, think you could say selfish,' said Lucy. 'But also it was as if they were just too busy doing the job they were given, keeping their heads down. And a lot of the very bad stuff like diseases and droughts and starvation that was happening because of the climate mainly happened to really poor people. They didn't seem to have a way of getting themselves noticed or heard at all.'

'And then around 2030 lots of bad stuff started to happen really quickly everywhere to everyone. It all like *accelerated*. It reminded me a bit of when we tried to stop the dike bursting in the spring. We plugged one hole, but another one appeared. We just had to let that bottom field go. It was a shame, but at least we had other fields we could use. The trouble was that they just kind of ran out of fields.'

Anna could hear the weariness in her voice. She was young. It was times like this she needed her Mum. 'Sounds like you're doing a great job, love. At least you've got no shortage of stuff for a story,' she said, aware how lame that sounded but trying at least to be reassuring.

'Too right, that's the problem really, there's too much. I've created something on the laptop, a folder, and started to collect the different information in it. I'm going to have to sort it all, but first I just thought I'd put stuff that seemed important together and get it all into some sort of timeline. Look.'

Lucy took out the notebook she had been scribbling in and read out what she had written under the title 'Warning Signs.'

In 2020 people knew that:

- *global warming was changing sea temperatures and melting ice caps*
- *pesticides with nasty chemicals were entering the food chain*
- *land was being over farmed*
- *eco tourism holidays were taking people to see animals that were dying out*
- *movies based on predictions of various environmental threats were popular*
- *there was increased Northern Lights activity: evidence of solar wind that would eventually knock out satellites and destroy electricity generation*
- *there were risks of a lack of power in places totally reliant on oil based energy for heat, light, cooking, air conditioning*
- *there was not enough attention to creating alternative fuel sources*
- *there were more geological disturbances such as earthquakes and tsunamis*
- *auto immune related conditions in the developed world were on the increase, but there was little coherent addressing of environmental or lifestyle causes*
- *increased focus on profits for drug companies meant drugs were rationed to those that could pay*

As Lucy read through the list she could feel her pulse starting to race again. She was beginning to understand why Jude had been so dismissive of the efforts of the *20/20 Vision* team.

'I don't understand why more people didn't just join forces and do something' she said. 'That's what we'd do.'

They were silent, each processing this thought.

'Well, I guess it's easy with hindsight to say that, but maybe they were just too close to it all?' Anna sighed.

Seb was looking over the list. 'Yeah, but come on Mum, Lucy's right. These are big flashing hazard warning signs! They're like a lighthouse for goodness sake. You couldn't miss these.'

'I thought the same. There had to be a reason why things got worse. So I had a bit of a think, and then I realised someone must have got something out of all this otherwise they would have done more. So I typed this next question.' Turning over the paper Lucy read out the words she had scrawled there:

'Who profited from global warming?'

'And do you know what I found? Article after article about how countries with gas and oil got richer as other types of fuel got scarcer. There were loads of headlines about people who had power in those countries taking up positions on company boards and getting big pay checks. Sometimes they declared interests while they were in the public eye, sometimes they didn't. It was all pretty murky. People thought they had influence, maybe because of the friends they had or who they were connected with. Bit like if you were close to Jude here because he's such an important person in the

85

Community you'd maybe think you'd learn something useful by talking to him. They made money from that, because people paid them to go and talk to other people and get them what they wanted.'

'So it was really all about money and power?' said Seb bitterly.

'Sort of. And there were people called shareholders, they didn't ask too many questions, maybe because they benefitted too. Do you know what? I even found executives that did protest about what was going on getting intimidated or even dismissed. How bad is that? They were called '*whistle blowers*' because they made a lot of noise. Sometimes that got written about in newspapers or they made programmes about them. But almost always they got excluded or attacked. It was like they couldn't hide anywhere. It must have been very scary for them. I think some of them were really brave.'

Anna brought a bowl of apples to the table and selecting one took a bite, nodding to the other two to help themselves. Then Seb spoke up.

'There's something I don't understand. You know all these people that were making money from all this. What did they actually do to earn that money?'

Lucy's eyes shone and she rubbed her hands in her hair till it stood up in spikes. 'It's crazy. The thing is, most of the time they didn't 'do' anything, not in the way we mean 'do' anyway. They weren't the ones that went out and drilled for the oil or built refineries or delivered to petrol stations. They kind of were in the background, turning the wheels, but imaginary ones. They were sort of in the shadows.'

'But Lucy, doesn't there always have to be someone keeping things going behind the scenes?' asked Anna. 'I mean, we have Jude don't we? He kind of organises us and plans stuff. You could say he does our thinking while we do the work. But is it really like that? There are plenty of parents that say they're behind the scenes doing the thinking for their children. Seb, you'd never have anything clean to wear if I didn't think for you!'

Lucy thought hard for a moment. She was trying to get things straight in her head. She could see Anna's point. Everyone was so busy labouring in the Community just to stay alive. If Jude was not doing their thinking for them and their planning then who would? And he kept saying he had given lots of thought to Duty Calls, far more than she had ever done. She was convinced he had all of their best interests at heart, but something still did not add up quite right for her.

Seb broke the silence. 'You know Mum, I don't mind you doing my washing or checking I'm eating properly. Well, not most of the time anyway! Because you're my Mum.' He paused for a moment. 'I guess I trust you. But I hate it when I feel like you're telling me what to do, not letting me make my own decisions. That's what Jude does all the time. He's not my Dad and he doesn't have anyone to answer to. It's just him. He's basically nothing more than a dictator.'

Anna frowned. 'It's funny, I used to say exactly the same when I was your age. I thought my parents were nagging me. I hated it when they said they were only telling me stuff *for my own good*. They thought they knew best. But who were they to tell me? After all it was my life!'

'The trouble is, when you get to be a parent you see it all differently. You love your children. You've got experience, you do know stuff. You can't bear to see your child hurt, you want to protect them, and in a way you want to protect yourself too. If anything happened to your child you'd be devastated. And if for one second you thought you could have done something to stop that bad thing happening, you'd never forgive yourself. You're responsible, like Jude's responsible. So you have to say something.'

'Blimey!'

Anna sighed. 'I know. It's crazy isn't it? There you are, happily going along through life and then you have a child. And, all of a sudden your entire happiness is tied up in this little person that is so vulnerable and reliant on you. It's bad enough when they're babies but once they get a bit older and start making their own decisions it's much worse because we all think we're indestructible when we're young. When I think of all the times I've chased round after you Seb, stopping you falling over, burning yourself, getting sick. It's exhausting.'

'So why do it?'

'That's easy. I do it because I love you. You're my son.'

Lucy wandered over to the window and watched the pinpoints of starlight that were beginning to appear in the deep darkness outside. She was quiet for a moment, trying to get things straight in her mind. She stuck her hands in her pockets and rested her forehead wearily on the window.

'I can see that Jude has a sense of responsibility towards us all. I can understand that parents want to protect their children. That's their job after all, to keep their children happy and safe. None of us asks to be born. If I was a Mum I'd always be there for my child. But with a parent you trust that what they're doing is meant to make you happy, keep you safe. What do you do when someone that's supposed to be looking out for you, like a Mum or Dad, does something that they think is right for you, but isn't what you think is right?'

Anna took a deep breath. She knew this was about Erin. She had no idea if anything she said would make things better, or worse.

'There's no rule book for parenting, Lucy. Most of us just work on instinct, make it up as we go along and muddle through. In a way we have tunnel vision. We're so focused on what's in front of us and keeping our child safe that we don't always see the bigger picture.'

Lucy took a few minutes to process this and then something suddenly seemed to make sense.

'Yes, I can see how that happens with parents. But Seb's right. I don't think people with responsibility like Jude have a right to make decisions for us or to tell us what we can and can't do.'

'It's different with parents though Lucy. They love their children.'

She had her answer. 'Love isn't just about control though is it, Anna? You remember that thing Mum used to say when I hurt myself? She didn't tell me off for trying something new. She used to say if I didn't fall down sometimes, I'd never learn how to get up.'

It was later that week that she put her finger on what she was thinking. Maybe love wasn't just about keeping you safe. Maybe it was really more to do with letting you go? Was that what Jude thought the Duty Calls sacrifice was meant to be about: letting go?

To be honest though, when it was someone you really cared about who needed you, she couldn't see what was so wrong about holding on.

Dilemmas

Over the next week Lucy found herself as she went about her daily chores turning over everything she, Anna and Seb had talked about that night. She could not understand why her forebears had not done more to stop problems getting worse. True, there had been demonstrations and arguments in governments, but it was all so complicated to try to put right. And no one could seem to agree about what 'right' would look like. It almost felt like some people just didn't want things to change.

She could also see that, unlike the way the Community was organised, resources in the past were not shared equally. Food for example, something the Community really prized, had been wasted in some parts of the world. In other places where the climate made it difficult to grow food, or there were problems like wars and no roads or railways to move it from one area to another, people were starving.

She talked with Seb one Sunday as they made their way up and down the rows of apple trees in a secluded valley a mile or so from home. Ordinarily she enjoyed this work, selecting the ripe fruit carefully, packing it into the wooden crates that they used to store and preserve the apples in cool cellars under some of the cottages.

'Jude works hard for us,' she said as they made their way down the rows. 'We chose him to be our leader. He sees himself as having authority and responsibility, but also being here to serve the Community.'

'He's in charge, for sure,' said Seb bitterly. 'I've told you, he's a dictator. I hate how he thinks he's got everything worked out. He talks to us like we're idiots sometimes. He's answerable to no one but himself. No one challenges him. He just does what he wants.'

Lucy felt really uncomfortable. Was Jude a dictator? Or did he just know best? She could not decide.

'Are you excited to be chosen?' asked Seb after a while, not looking at her.

'You jealous?'

'Course not! Don't be daft.'

Maybe she *was* enjoying the attention. The way Jude studied her made her feel special. She was not just Lucy the poor little orphan any more. She had respect, responsibilities and, because it was Jude who had chosen her, a halo of authority over her work.

She glanced across at her cousin as he toiled. She loved Seb and didn't want to fall out with him. There was only a few months difference in their ages and they had grown up more like brother and sister than cousins. Admittedly she did not know many other boys her age, but she always felt Seb was special. Talking to him was so different from talking to her Mum or Anna. He was always direct and incisive, but he could be incredibly tender and caring towards her. She never really thought of him as a boy. He was just Seb, her cousin, her champion, her friend.

She had joked about it when she was little. 'When I'm grown up I'm going to marry Seb and have babies.' Her Mum had laughed. 'You can't marry Seb, he's your cousin. But you can always be friends.'

That was everything to her. She trusted him completely. Anna said he thought more like a girl than a boy and she could tell she knew they had a special sort of relationship. He always seemed to have intuition, to know instinctively what to do to help her, how to be or who to trust.

And he never seemed interested in 'boy stuff.' He would far rather read a book or talk than take part in any of the rough and tumble or more macho activities that were in such abundance in the Community. He always sought out her company or Anna's, never the other young lads that lived round about. You could tell some of them thought that a bit strange, but he did not seem to care. He knew who and what he was and was comfortable in that knowledge. And because he was comfortable he made Lucy comfortable too.

They had worked hard till late afternoon and she was coming back from the fields, deep in thought and trying to prepare herself for the next day's visit to the crypt. Seb had chosen to stay and finish up, and she had offered to go home and start supper. Turning a corner, she was surprised to see Jude coming out of the church. He greeted her kindly and they fell into step as they crossed the churchyard together. It was a beautiful warm afternoon and he indicated a bench nestled under an overhanging tree branch where they could sit and take in the scene that stretched ahead of them down to the sea.

'Are you ready for your next session with the Time Capsule tomorrow?' he asked.

'Sort of,' said Lucy.

'What's wrong my child?' Jude turned to face Lucy and placed a hand on her knee. 'You look troubled. Would it help to talk?'

Somehow she could not help herself. With a deep sigh everything she had been struggling with tumbled out.

'I just don't get it,' she said. 'I guess I didn't realise till last week just how greedy and thoughtless and selfish everyone used to be. I hadn't expected that. And it's making me feel angry.'

'Surely not everyone was selfish?' said Jude. 'Have you not found any examples of countries learning to work together or caring about the impact of what they were doing? Sometimes it's easier to solve the smaller problems close to home than try to tackle something that's really big and complicated you know.'

Lucy was silent for a moment. 'Mmm, I'll maybe have a think about that for tomorrow. Thanks Jude.'

They sat in silence, listening to the gentle lapping of the incoming tide on the shoreline. Keeping his eyes fixed on the distant horizon Jude finally broke Lucy's train of thought.

'One of the things history teaches us, Lucy, is how human beings haven't really changed that much over the centuries. Our environment alters of course. Sometimes we have lots of resources, sometimes less. Sometimes we know a lot about why things happen, sometimes we can't see any reason, or can't make sense of the evidence. But we've always had the same basic needs: to be fed and sheltered, to be loved, to feel safe, to belong and to be treated fairly. From that perspective some things never change. Maybe...' and here Jude emphasised his purpose by drumming his fist on her knee in time to his words, '...people sometimes just feel the need to have their turn to live the way they want to. That's only natural. The question is, is it wise?'

Not for the first time Lucy could feel her brain aching. It was so complicated. Just when she thought she had understood everything that had happened, something else came to light that made her have to think again. She was realising this was not going to be a simple 'goodies' and 'baddies' story to tell.

After a short silence Jude spoke. 'This may seem an odd thing to ask, Lucy, but I am wondering, has all this investigating made you think about the value of work at all? Work is something we put great store on here in the Community as you know. It gives purpose and meaning to our lives because everything we do links to our survival. Is there anything you've noticed about the way work was thought about in the past that feels different from how we think about it today?'

Lucy pondered hard on this. How was work viewed in the past? There were the various ways people could earn a living, the way some people did not work but still got money to live, the fact that some people earned huge amounts and others did not get much at all. What was it that was so different about work then and work now in the Community?

Suddenly a light bulb exploded in her head.

'Of course. We don't work for money.'

Jude smiled indulgently down at her. 'Exactly, Lucy. We don't work for money. So what do we work for?'

'We work for each other.'

'And in what ways does that make a difference?'

Lucy had to think about this one. 'Well, for one thing we only produce what we really need. We try to make sure there's just enough to go round and if we have anything left over we share it out.'

Jude nodded. 'Does the fact that we know how vulnerable we are matter?'

'I guess it makes us all feel more responsible maybe. You always do your work and you don't waste time or food because you know if you did then we'd all suffer.'

'Quite. We are a relatively small group and we know each other well so it's hard to let each other down. Tell me, did you see people suffering in the past?'

She certainly had. She had seen people really hungry and cold and sick. Most of these lived in other countries, which meant it would be difficult to understand them like you would people in your own neighbourhood. But some of the really poor people lived right in the middle of very rich cities where people had far more than they could ever need, while they slept outdoors on the street and had to beg for food.

And not everyone was kind or particularly respectful to these people. She had read one newspaper article where it had been suggested that some people had brought all this hardship on themselves and did not deserve to be helped. What did it say? *'Don't give money to these people for they will only spend it on drugs and alcohol.'* She had thought at the time that sounded pretty unfair. After all, those in charge were not exactly perfect either.

'I get the feeling that people didn't understand each other as well as we do in the Community,' she said. 'I guess that had to make a difference. Maybe it's easier to ignore someone that you don't really know or can't really see.'

'Or someone that looks different? Or speaks a different language so it's hard to communicate and understand what they are feeling?'

'Yes, I guess so.'

She had also seen lots of people in her research that could not work. They were too ill, or too young or too old. They were often looked after, not just by families but by people whose job it was to do that. And she had even seen individuals that would never be able to work again or were actually dying being cared for. She shivered. She knew that would never happen in the Community

'They used to have all sorts of people to help you if you were ill or needed support. It must have been amazing to have lived back then. You'd have felt so safe and secure compared with how we feel.

But then those people that worked in places that protected you, like schools or hospitals or helped you to find somewhere to live gradually seemed to disappear. I don't really understand why that happened or where they all went. It just seems like one minute they were there and then all of a sudden a few years later they were gone. What happened to them do you think? They couldn't just vanish could they?'

'My father and Nick spoke about this many times as I was growing up,' said Jude. 'My father, ever the pragmatist, argued that as resources got tighter they simply couldn't afford to be collectively responsible for everyone in the way they had been. Nick, however, always said we should love our neighbours like we loved our own families. My father used to think that was naive. Everyone would always put their own families first; it's human nature to do so.'

'How would you ever decide who your neighbours were?'

'That was exactly my father's point. So instead he believed everyone had to learn to stand on their own two feet more. But for some people it was easier to be independent and secure because they were healthier or smarter or had a more supportive family or money from the beginning. And these lucky ones weren't necessarily the most hard working or honest or kindest. On the contrary, sometimes they were really greedy and they'd got their money by committing crimes or doing things that hurt others a lot.'

'There were always discussions in my house about all this. Hope and I grew up hearing these arguments. Our parents thought world leaders often focused on things that scared them, like terrorism, but with hindsight, they arguably should have done more about the environment. I mean it's obvious really. If there's less land to grow food then people have to either starve, or move away, or invest in different ways of producing food, or you have to find a way to reduce the population. If they'd paid more attention to that then maybe they'd have recognised sooner just how pressing was the need for everyone to adapt their behaviour.'

'Instead, as resources got tighter, and the world was perceived as scarier, nations started to withdraw into themselves and look after those they saw as their own. Time was lost and resources diverted into defence and self protection rather than working together to come up with global solutions. Part of me thinks as the dangers got closer people felt they couldn't stop them and some just buried their heads in the sand.'

Jude paused. When he next spoke it was as if Lucy was not there and he was talking to himself.

'Our parents, grandparents and even great grandparents could have done far more. They walked blindly along, not responding to the warning signs. I cannot decide if this came from selfish disregard or, perhaps more charitably, simply a sense of being overwhelmed by the enormity of what was happening, a feeling of powerlessness to make a difference because the realities were just too unimaginable to countenance.'

Again he hesitated, and then seemed to remember where he was.

'One thing however is undeniable, Lucy, and I am sure you will see this as you carry on with your task. Anyone that had access to the internet could not have failed to be aware at some level that something needed to be done. I can draw no other conclusion from what my father and Nick talked about. I cannot understand why they did not do more. It was surely their duty to do so.'

The sun was gradually setting and the day was drawing to its close. Lucy felt weary and she thought Jude also looked tired. He seemed to read her thoughts.

'This role has taken its toll on me Lucy, I cannot deny that. As you know, I have been Chief Steward here for a long time. I have always striven to do my duty to our Community. The task is not without its challenges or its burdens. I do not say this to complain or to boast. It is simply a fact.'

Jude paused and studied Lucy briefly, appearing to be reassuring himself that she was being attentive to his words. Satisfied that he had her complete attention, he continued.

'In the past, for an estate to function properly, the steward needed to hold *himself* accountable for all that took place in the household. He might delegate, but he would maintain an interest in all happenings, make it his duty to know all of the operational details, when to intervene and when to concentrate on other matters. He would need to gather information, both from reports by the staff and from actual inspection of the estate.'

'Like your files in your cottage?' said Lucy

'Exactly, like my files. The best steward would be the one who felt the responsibility on the deepest level, who identified with the role and carried it out with devoted industry. I have tried to live up to that standard and be that sort of role model.'

As Lucy listened she began to realise the extent to which Jude's personality was entirely suited to the role he was outlining. Here was someone for whom accountability, attention to detail, information and tenacious diligence were touchstones, measures that defined his identity. They ran through him like the yearly growth lines in a tree trunk. They were the characteristics that provided the channels through which nutrients flowed that, in turn, contributed to creating the person she saw before her now. Maybe Jude did not need a team or a council after all. Perhaps he was just clever enough to make decisions for the Community on his own?

For a long moment they sat in silence. 'Come, my child,' said Jude eventually getting to his feet. He stood very close to her, almost touching. She could see every detail of the black stubble on his face. Lucy held her breath and without realising it, bit hard into her bottom lip to stop it from trembling. He looked down on her, breathing heavily. 'You are very special to me Lucy. One day I believe you will be very special to the whole Community.'

' Now, I have kept you too long. Go home and rest. You have much to do tomorrow.'

That night Lucy sat with Anna and Seb unfolding what she and Jude had talked about. When she had finished Anna sat thoughtfully, looking into the dying embers of the fire as Seb poked it to tease out the last of its warmth. Lucy decided not to mention that Jude had said she was 'special.' She did not want to rile Seb.

'In some ways I wish I had Jude's conviction. He just believes 100% that he is right.'

'Jude really wants to protect the Community,' said Anna. 'No one could say he doesn't. So what is it that makes you still feel so uncomfortable about Duty Calls?'

'I know what it is,' said Seb, playing with the fire. 'You don't want someone you care about to be judged and found wanting because we all know what happens then.' He stabbed the poker hard into a log, smashing it to pieces and sending a shower of sparks up the chimney. 'And it's not our decision or our family's, it's bloody Jude's.'

Lucy looked thoughtful. That was maybe it. Things were so different with Duty Calls when you were talking about someone you loved.

On the third day

Lucy spent all week churning over and over the questions arising from her conversations with Jude, Anna and Seb. She had tossed and turned most nights, not rising refreshed, feeling instead even more tired than when she had gone to bed. Every day her normal chores had required greater effort than usual. Her head ached with confused feelings and bitter resentments. She had time to think as she joined the other young women sitting at the shoreline mending nets each day.

'You're miles away, Lucy,' teased Scarlett. 'I've asked you three times to pass the basket over. Is it a lad?'

Lucy blushed. 'Don't be daft,' she snorted and heaved the wicker container where the nets were packed away for the winter over to her. 'I was just thinking, that's all.'

However, waking on the morning of what would be her third day of working on the Project, Lucy sensed inside her a new determination. In many ways it was a relief to be going back to work. Being at the laptop would give opportunities to direct her thoughts and emotions into something purposeful. Maybe she was overthinking it all and just creating problems that weren't even there.

'It doesn't really matter why I'm feeling like this,' she said to Lela, nuzzling her face in her fur as she waited for the water to boil in the pan over the fire to make her morning tea. 'I just need to face up to these feelings and get on with it.'

So when, a short while later, Lucy found herself settling once again into the high backed chair in the crypt she knew exactly what she was going to ask the programme next. She turned on the laptop and with rapidly moving fingers typed the question she had prepared into the search box.

'Did anyone in the 20th and 21st centuries care about communities?'

What Lucy found out in the next few hours amazed and deeply disturbed her. It was not what she had been expecting. Rather than finding evidence of not caring, she had no idea that it was possible to care so much.

What staggered her as she worked was the sheer amount of support that there had been for vulnerable, older and disabled people in her great grandparents' day. She uncovered names of hundreds of organisations and charities working in towns, cities and villages up and down the country. They were staffed, typically, by a mixture of paid workers and volunteers. Almost every conceivable health issue, learning difficulty, physical disability, mental health matter was, to various degrees, catered for. There was support for individuals, families, young people, old people, babies, children, intergenerational work. Help was available in people's homes, local neighbourhoods, in specially constructed or adapted buildings, over the phone or the internet and, in many cases all day and night.

What drove these workers to make such a commitment to people that were not family or even friends? She lost count of the number of events she came across that people organised and took part in to raise cash. Often there was very little improvement in the condition of the people being helped. In fact 'caring' meant simply looking after their most basic needs for feeding, washing, dressing, toileting in order to make them comfortable until they died. She was only too well aware that this would never happen in the Community.

She was intrigued by these people, especially the volunteers. What made them act like this? What was in it for them? To Lucy's eyes, this level of care seemed intensely challenging and heroic, but at the same time extraordinarily short sighted.

Pushing back from the table after almost two hours of research, she wrenched open the door and paced around the church walking up and down the stone flagged aisle. Saints and apostles stared down at her from ancient leaded windows, but she was oblivious to the archaic carvings and decorations that surrounded her. She gained no comfort from them. All she felt was agitation and confusion.

On the one hand she had nothing but admiration for the extent to which people and organisations in the past were willing to go in order to help those that life had dealt a cruel hand. Whether it was motivated by pity, empathy or something else, deep inside her she could not escape a feeling that it was incredibly worthy, even noble, to show such compassion. But she also had an uneasy feeling that this energy and sympathy could, with the benefit of hindsight, have been better directed given that at the same time the clock had been ticking down rapidly on so much else on the planet.

She sat on one of the old wooden pews facing the spot where once the priest must have conducted services for the gathered congregation, turning all this over in her mind. The table that stood on the raised dais was bare where there had probably at one time been a cross. Lucy found herself staring vacantly forward, trying to understand what she was seeing.

She stretched out her legs and propped them up on the back of the pew in front of her, clasping her hands behind her head and leaning backwards. As she pondered, her eyes roamed around the church interior, taking in the weathered stonework and the dust motes dancing in the rays pouring through the windows. Eventually she came to focus on the huge stained glass window in the wall behind the altar. It was very beautiful. The design was a kaleidoscope of blue and green glass, echoing the colours of the landscape of the island she knew so well. She had never really paid much attention to it before but now she studied it carefully, conscious of the skill it must have taken to construct it, taking in the way the sunlight streamed through and pooled in rainbow mosaics on the floor in front of her.

Beneath the window was a large grey stone plaque set in the wall. It was the first time she had noticed it. There were some faint indentations in it, just visible to the naked eye if you looked really closely. Lowering her feet she wandered over, hands in pockets, to take a better look. The carvings were words, covered in a thick layer of dust, but still just about able to be seen peeping through. She started to brush away the fine powder with her fingertips, gently coaxing the letters beneath into view and gradually revealing a text which she eventually was able to decipher:

But when you give a feast, invite the poor, the crippled, the lame, the blind, and you will be blessed, because they cannot repay you. For you will be repaid at the resurrection of the just.
Luke 14:13-14

'They cannot repay you, but you will be repaid,' she murmured to herself. And turning she walked slowly out of the church and made her way down to a secluded corner of the churchyard.

This time there was no Jude to share her thoughts with, and even Lela was otherwise engaged helping Seb with the rounding up of the sheep scattered around the island. It was down to her. She found a slab of rock covered in moss and took out her notebook where she had been scribbling down thoughts and findings as she had been working that morning.

She had been focusing her search around the period between 2015 and 2020. There had been lots of talk about the need to live according to the means available, especially as people were living longer so that more demands were being made on the resources available. She found a quote from someone that she assumed must have been a politician or civil servant, *'As a country, we simply can't afford this level of welfare anymore.'* She wondered whose perception this had been and who was making the decisions about how the money was being spent. The country had looked very rich to her.

That night she tried to explain it to Seb and Anna. 'I can just about understand why 'deserving' people got help because they at least might pay you back.'

'You mean there was a good chance that you'd get a return on the investment?' said Seb

'Well, that's not a nice way to think about it, but, yes, I guess that's it really. At least you knew there'd be some reward for all the effort. What I can't understand is why they put so much energy into people that were never going to be able to repay them and weren't expected to give anything back. And some people seemed just to rely on the community as if it was their right. And even though they could choose to live and eat healthily why did some people choose to do things that weren't good for them? Didn't they have some responsibility themselves?'

'And as antibiotics stopped working so well they don't seem to have got to the bottom of why that was happening either. Was it that the bacteria were adapting so our bodies couldn't defend against them?'

'Finding out that stuff was surely more important than just patching people up?' said Seb.

Lucy went very quiet. 'I know. It made me think about Mum and Dad. There probably wasn't much that would have saved Dad from his heart attack. But Mum was different. We never really found out what her virus was. Let's face it by the time she died there were a few things it could have been. But from what I can see from the Time Capsule people seemed to be noticing that something was messing with all of our immune systems for ages. New viruses kept emerging that they just couldn't keep ahead of with drugs but they tried to find out why some people were more resistant than others. And something could have been making us more susceptible. Was it all the pesticides in the food chain or the chemicals in the water or the pollutants in the air? Was there anything they could have done or do we just have to accept that we all have to die of something?'

Anna could feel her eyes welling up and she had to look away. She did not want to say it, but she thought Lucy might have a point. Was it possible that if her grandparents' generation had understood more and been able to intervene then Erin might still have been with them?

'I was thinking about Grandpa and Grandma. They always talked like people that didn't have the stuff they had were just short sighted or lazy or must have been wasteful.'

'Yes, but don't forget they'd never known any different,' said Anna. 'Mum and Dad were both from pretty well off families. They'd never had to worry about money. Thinking about it, they probably didn't know anyone that was really poor. It was only when they got ill themselves that they would have realised how much they needed other people. But I guess when that happened they always had family, me and your Mum, to look after them.'

'I can really see what Jude meant about it not always being the nicest people or the ones that worked hardest that had the most resources.' said Lucy. 'There were people trying to raise money for what I suppose you'd call 'good causes' and they didn't seem to get as much support as they deserved, to be honest. There was plenty of talk about needing to make the world a fairer place, but I just couldn't see much evidence of that really happening.'

All this thinking came later however. For now, after sitting in the churchyard for a while, Lucy felt she had got nowhere on her own and she was only too well aware that time was pressing and that she needed to get on with the task in hand. Eventually she put her notebook away with a sigh.

Making her way home she reported in to Jude as usual. He listened intently to her account of what she had found out and as she finished a long silence descended over the room. When he finally spoke it was as if he was dragging a story up from deep within his own memory and re-examining it forensically for clues and answers.

'We really do not have the luxury of these debates, Lucy, I'm afraid. Time is of the essence now and I need you to focus on the job in hand. Our ancestors had opportunities that are not afforded to us. Perhaps it simply all boils down to one question: *What's right and what's fair*? My Uncle Nick advocated fiercely for the poor and the needy on many occasions when he and my father discussed these matters. My father was not however sure that an individual should expect a community to look after them unless they were prepared to put something back themselves.'

'There's a verse from the Bible carved into the church wall,' Lucy said. 'I'd never seen it before. Hang on, let me find it.' She rifled through her notebook and read out the words she had copied down from the stone plaque into it. 'You believe in Heaven don't you Jude? Does that verse mean we should care for people that can't work themselves because when we die we'll get our reward in Heaven?'

Jude looked thoughtful and seemed to be turning all of these questions over. 'You want life to be fair Lucy. But something you learn as you get older is that it just isn't. Inequality and unfairness is just everywhere. Some people are born lucky, some are not. And there's no rhyme or reason for that. Shakespeare had something to say about this: *'As flies to wanton boys, are we to the gods, they kill us for their sport.'* He meant that our fate is in the lap of the gods. Did you know that's where the word *handicapped* comes from? When you put your hand in a cap you get whatever you draw out. Our choices rest in how we choose to respond to whatever straw we draw or hand we've been dealt. Do we look after ourselves, hope to stay lucky and survive, or do we strive to redress the balance for those that are less fortunate?'

'In Old Testament times there would have been a fear that if you sinned you would be punished and be sent to a place which they called Hell. People had an assurance that one day, if they did good deeds, they would be rewarded in Heaven.'

'It's certainly helpful I feel to believe in an afterlife. It provides a justification for helping people that can't contribute to the Community any more on and into it. But to my eyes our Community simply does not have the luxury to be able to 'feast' the poor, the crippled, the lame or the blind. Our forebears had their chance to preserve a world where that would be possible, but they failed to do so. And in my view, those rules or ways of being are simply luxuries we can no longer afford.'

That night Lucy once again thumbed through her notes with Anna and Seb and realised she was just starting to see faint glimmers of blurry patterns emerging through the dark clouds in her mind.

'You know what it is, Lucy?' Seb said eventually as the pair of them stretched out on the old sofa, having talked till it was nightfall and stars were appearing, like tiny glow worms through the window in the sky above them. 'Maybe the people that worked with the poor, the crippled, the lame and the blind in the olden days and believed in Heaven just thought about Community very differently. It all sounds very noble but maybe for them everyone was their neighbour. It didn't matter what someone could do or couldn't do. Maybe some of them weren't thinking about getting a reward in some sort of Heaven either. Yes, they had their other motivations, they got paid or it made them feel good about themselves. But at the heart of it and maybe not in a way that they thought about every day, what drove some of them to make real sacrifices was that they believed everyone just had a right to be cared for, because they were human beings. That's maybe what Jude doesn't get. We didn't have to meet some 'standard.' We were connected. We were all one family. It was simple. Everyone mattered and everyone just belonged.'

On the fourth day

All that week Lucy pondered on everything that working on the Time Capsule was teaching her. It was her turn to do some childcare. Preparations for the Ceremony were progressing, and although it was still a good few weeks away, everyone was talking about what Jude might have in mind. The girls chattered about little else as they cared for the youngest children.

'He says there's going to be a time full of big surprises and that it's going to be a night we'll never forget,' said Scarlett excitedly as they all pulled coats and hats on before going home for the day. 'I can't wait! What do you think he's planning for us?'

Beyond the presentation of her story, Lucy had no idea. The more she had explored, the more she was coming to perceive the world of her parents and grandparents as confused. In some ways selfish, in others extraordinarily compassionate towards people like her Mum who would never 'pay back', people who would not fare well in the Community.

It was now October and she was supposed to be gathering information to tell a story at a New Year's Eve event in less than three months time. It had to be a history of how the world had become as it was, in spite of all the warning signs of an impending global disaster. If she was going to get that task completed she needed to get on with it.

So, it was with genuine curiosity and a sense of some urgency that on the fourth day she settled herself into the now familiar chair and typed her next question into the search engine: *'Did anyone in 2020 have a vision for the future?'*

Up came lists of information instantly in a whole range of different formats produced in the run up to what she soon realised were national elections. Foremost amongst these articles and podcasts was a YouTube of a speech entitled *'2020 Vision'* given to her surprise, by a much younger, but immediately recognisable, Nick Grigori.

It was a short film in the style of a party political broadcast. It had all the feel of something produced by student activists. It was raw, but passionate and powerful, the opening shots interspersed with images of drought ridden land, people sleeping in doorways, closed hospitals, dilapidated schools. There was no doubting the message. Things were getting worse and something had to be done.

Nick's voiceover described a future where the world's population had been almost obliterated by a whole range of predictable financial, medical and global environmental disasters. Lucy shivered. The description almost exactly matched her reality.

'There is every chance that the remnants of the human race will be pushed back to an island community so vulnerable that only the youngest and fittest can survive in it. What would happen to those that were more in need, the elderly, the vulnerable, the disabled? They would be regarded as worthless commodities, passengers. Think of the impact this would have on our sense of

humanity. We need to act now to stop this happening. One day it will be too late to turn back the clock.'

The film then cut to what was clearly meant to remind the viewer of a rather bland and corporate government information broadcast. To the sound of gently piped music the words *'Welcome to our local Duty Calls Centre'* appeared on screen. The camera ranged over a building she recognised from pictures her grandparents had shown her of holidays they had been on. It was an airport. Signs directing passengers to the 'Departure Lounge' and then various 'Gates' were interspersed by what she assumed must have been studio shots where 'passengers' took identity documents to smiling, efficient looking officials and were then invited either to sit in the waiting areas or waved through to smaller rooms or windows for 1:1 interviews.

As she watched the film, papers were stamped and the passengers, or as the voice over described them, 'consumers' passed from one Gate to the next. Each Gate had images in its waiting area reflecting the stage of life an individual might expect to be at when they reached that point in their journey through them. The voice over spoke in warm and reassuring tones about the careful assessing of an individual's capacities and capabilities at each Gate and the matching of work assignments to the abilities ('resources') that 'consumer' could bring.

'Oh my God, this is Duty Calls!' Lucy's words bounced round the tiny crypt and made Lela jump. She had been so absorbed in what she was doing that she had completely forgotten where she was.

She watched the screen as a man, who was clearly not well, shuffled into the Departure Lounge and was told to report to Gate 19 (a line of numbers told the viewer that there were only 20 Gates in total). He moved slowly and, judging by the look on his face, apparently with considerable pain. The camera panned over the other elderly and disabled people at Gate 19, all sitting waiting, several with obvious signs of infirmity like crutches and wheelchairs.

The man was shown entering an 'Assessment Room.' The door was opened by someone dressed as a doctor, revealing a brief glimpse of a hospital bed and medical instruments. When he emerged the doctor was smiling warmly and reassuringly while the man carried a folder stamped 'Final Assignment.' Still to the sound of gentle music he was then taken by the arm by an official. She pointed down the corridor to a separate area labelled Gate 20.

A voice over explained that Gate 20 was the entrance to the Duty Calls hospice where *consumers* that could no longer *benefit* the community would spend their last day. The man appeared to accept his final destination willingly with an air of total resignation. As he walked through Gate 20 he was presented with a certificate that congratulated him for his responsible approach to citizenship. While he disappeared through the door in a haze of cloudy dry ice the camera panned to a video screen showing a 'Duty Calls' march past where old, infirm and disabled people were being applauded. Lucy felt sick. All she could think about was her Mum.

116

The broadcast went back to Nick's voice speaking over pictures of a beach, wide open, sandy, the early morning sunshine turning the sea into countless glittering diamonds. A few people were walking their dogs, throwing balls for them to chase into the water or along the sand. A toddler in red wellies, pink cheeked with bunched curls pinned haphazardly under a too cute hat ran almost to the water's edge and then turned and scurried back to her mother screaming giddily as the waves came towards her. The woman gathered her into wide open arms and swung her round in the sunshine.

Nick's voice cut through the images. *'Do you think these people are somehow different from those that you might see scrabbling and pushing and fighting for food or water or living space for themselves and their families? Isn't all that makes them different the availability of resources? 100 places on a boat leaving a sinking ship with 50 passengers, we get an orderly queue. I fear that with 100 places and 500 passengers we get a mob, carnage.'*

'It's up to us,' Nick said. *'What kind of Community do we want? Because right now we have freedom and we have choice, but in the future, if we carry on the way we are going, Duty Calls could become a reality. We can choose to use up the world and the resources in it as some sort of entitlement or we can nurture the planet with fairness and intelligence and maintain it as a gift for our children and our children's children.'*

'Are we commodities, raw material to be consumed and expended till, our energies exhausted, we are poured, literally, down

117

the drain? I do not think so. I believe each and every one of us, not
because of what we do but because of what we are, has value as well
as rights and responsibilities. We have been given the gift of our
beautiful planet and of life and the responsibility to respect and
cherish both. But unless we work hard and manage this situation
how will we preserve it?'

Lucy found herself dry mouthed, staring at the screen. Here
was a nightmare version of Duty Calls that was framed very
differently from the one that Jude had presented. She was intrigued
by Nick, by his opinions, but also by how he had managed to
achieve such prophetic insights. His ability to see the future
astounded her, but his analysis of what to do to change it was what
really intrigued her.

She arrived at Jude's cottage that evening deep in thought.
Rather than go in she seated herself on the bench outside, watching
the sun dropping slowly behind the distant hills and the sky starting
to pink up. After a few moments she heard a door open behind her
and footsteps approaching. She dragged her eyes from the sunset.

'You are finished for the day?' Jude asked, searching her
face to try to read her mood. 'Shall we debrief here or would you
rather come inside?'

Lucy looked back to the sky and took a deep breath. 'It's a
beautiful evening,' she said. 'I want to stay here.'

Jude settled on the bench beside her. 'As you wish. '

They sat for a few moments in silence. This was not a
companionable silence of shared pleasure though. It was merely a

pregnant pause before she knew she would need to report on her day's work.

They discussed her findings, but she made no mention of the extent to which she had explored Nick's philosophy. She answered Jude's enquiries politely, but briefly. Something made her wary and it did occur to her that Jude might know more than he was giving away. Surely the Duty Calls name was too much of a coincidence for him not to have some inkling of what Nick's views about it had been?

Making her excuses, Lucy handed over the key to the crypt as usual and hurried home. Jude watched her till she turned the corner and then stood staring at the empty space where she had been. He appeared deep in thought as, turning, he made his way back to the cottage. But, rather than going in, he pulled the door shut and instead headed off in the direction of the church.

On the fifth day

It was mid October. Over the week the weather had really started to change. There was a light frost one morning and the windows of the cottage were covered with icy fronds that Lucy had to scrape at with her fingers to make a small peephole to look through onto the frozen world beyond. Anna had been sorting through their winter clothes and each night she, Seb and Lucy had worked mending and patching both of their cottages' walls and roofs, making them as weatherproof as they could.

She had been trying each day to square the belief that her parents and grandparents had loved her with the extent to which they had lived in the present and perhaps not grappled too much with the impact of what they were doing on the future. In the end she came to a decision on the very morning that she was going back to the crypt.

'I think Nick's the clue. If I get to know him better, that might help,' she mused to Lela.

So, having collected the key from Jude's cottage and made her way rapidly through the chilly landscape to the church she settled at the laptop, wrapping herself in the extra blanket she had brought. It was an easy question to type.

'*Who was Nick Grigori?*'

The search engine again instantly produced a number of options, but one stood out to her as of special interest: '*Nick Grigori: Family Blog.*'

In an instant she was transported back to a conversation she had had with her grandmother one afternoon over tea. Gran had been telling her about when she was a teenager. Lucy remembered looking at her grandmother's wrinkles and finding it hard to believe she had ever been that age.

'I was so self conscious and shy! I wanted to fit in, be like everyone else, but I just couldn't. I never seemed to have the right clothes or the right look, I was just a geek! I hated it!'

'I kept a blog. Everyone did in those days. I guess it was our way of presenting an image of ourselves as we wanted others to see us. But I hardly let anyone else see mine, just my closest friends, people I thought I could trust. And even then I mainly did that late at night and when I'd got my courage up with a drink or two!'

'Did Gramps read it?' Lucy had asked.

'Oh, I didn't get to know your Grandpa till a long time later,' she had smiled. 'By then I was much more grown up and sorted! Funny, those people I did share it with meant so much to me at the time, their opinions and whether they liked me or not. Now, well I wouldn't know them if we passed in the street.'

Nick's family had kept an online blog with pictures and video clips of themselves talking to camera and scenes that stretched from 2000. It started with an account of his parents' visit to London to see the celebrations for the start of the 21st century.

Lucy was enthralled by the scenes. They could not be more different from the upcoming celebrations for which the Community was preparing. Sarai, Nick's mother, was filmed watching a magnificent firework display over the Thames, making her way through thousands of people all out drinking and dancing. She was heavily pregnant.

'Gosh, that's little Nick in there!' thought Lucy. The clothes and hairstyles reminded her very much of the sorts of things she had seen in her great grandparents' photo albums that had been handed down through the family.

She flicked through more than an hour of footage and text. The images provided an insight into the Grigori family in a way that she could never have believed would be as revealing, touching or evocative of a time gone by. The *20/20 Vision* team must have guessed it would so often not be the big events that captured what the time was like, but the incidental everyday experiences and ways of being. The things that someone like her would 'see' would be events people at the time took for granted because then they were so commonplace.

The contrast between Lucy's day to day existence and what was played out on screen took her breath away. Things like cars, street lights, shops, cinemas, people playing and relaxing, walking dogs and keeping animals as pets, the amount of diversity of activity, kitchens filled with every conceivable electrical appliance, just the sheer newness and disposability of everything seemed extraordinary to her. It was not so much a contrast to the world she knew, as the complete antithesis. It was a different planet.

The blog consisted of a series of shots of individuals talking to camera, voxpops often delivered by Sarai, but interspersed with the occasional input from Nick's father, Abe. There were lots of photographs and video clips. First just of the two of them but then as time went on increasingly of Nick as a baby, then a toddler, and on into his increasingly self conscious teenage years. When he was five his sister Rachel had been born and later, when he was about ten, the exquisitely beautiful and clearly adored little sister, Mia.

She had arrived one bright spring morning. Lucy was transfixed by a clip where she lay, pink and cherubic, on Sarai's lap watched over by a clearly devoted big brother and bubbly older sister. Lucy was completely drawn into the intensely intimate and personal story that was being played out in front of her.

'I know it was something they wanted to share, but I felt a bit like I was spying,' she said to Seb later that week as they worked together to muck out Willow's stable.

'Lucy Daniel: the Peeping Tom,' he chuckled. 'You always were a nosy cow.'

She heaved a fork load of straw at him. 'Shut up, you! I'm trying to be serious here. It wouldn't have been so bad if I hadn't felt like they weren't showing me what they intended me to see. I wasn't seeing what they thought they were showing.'

'I have absolutely no idea what you are talking about.'

Nor did she really. It was something about what they chose to film, and how that now appeared to her. She knew the team had developed the Time Capsule to enable people that came afterwards to view the past through a different lens in the hope that they would take lessons forward into the future. They had had no idea what

123

aspects of the past would be preserved, or what elements would be gone forever. Some would appear mere anachronisms, but others would be viewed as tragic losses. The *20/20 Vision* team was not going to make those judgements; it was up to those that came afterwards to do that.

She sensed it would be a waste of time talking to Seb about this. Much as she loved him he was more direct and less keen to ponder than she was. Later that evening when she was with Anna she tried to put into words what it was that was so striking about the blog. Her aunt listened attentively as the two of them carefully packed recently harvested potatoes into crates for the winter.

'Was it the way the camera almost accidentally captured what to you seem special moments? Things you saw because they were so unusual to us, but that they didn't even notice because they were just so familiar they were taken for granted?'

'Yes! That's it exactly.' Sometimes maybe grown ups did have their uses after all. Lucy had known that Anna would be able to help her to see things clearly. 'They didn't realise just how special their everyday existence actually was. It was completely invisible to them. They took every aspect for granted. Boiling a kettle, hanging out together with no agenda, even the backchat round the table at breakfast with the radio playing in the background and Sarai singing along while she made toast and the kids ate. It was so ordinary to them, but to me it looked extraordinary.'

'How did it make you feel seeing all those experiences that we don't have any more?'

Lucy thought for a few seconds, turning the question over in her mind before answering.

'Sad. Not angry, just sad. If I said I was angry it sounds like I'm cross with them, like they did something wrong. I realised I couldn't blame them for being happy with the things they had, anyone would be. They weren't hurting anyone, it was the opposite. They were ensuring the people they cared about the most were happy. They believed that was their responsibility. They were there for each other just like we'd all want to be. They were just connected.'

'You're growing very wise in your old age, young Lucy,' Anna smiled. She knew she had rationalised dealing with her own anger towards her parents' lack of foresight long ago. Being angry implied resentment and blame and blame just created bitterness. And bitterness could eat away at your soul. Anna had no desire to waste one drop of what little energy she had on something so negative.

'So tell me about Mia.'

Lucy looked into the firelight, her eyes bright with tears.

'She was born perfect but she got ill...some sort of auto immune condition, like Mum. There'd been drugs that would have helped but by 2020 they were only available in certain areas and they didn't live in one of them. Sarai and Abe fought really hard for Mia. But when she died she left a massive hole that no one could fill.'

There was a long silence. Eventually and wearily Lucy spoke. 'I know everyone is different, but I guess I knew what they felt like because of Mum.'

Anna put her arm round Lucy and held her close, her slender body feeling fragile. 'I know. When someone you love goes before they should it's like a hand grabs your heart, squeezes it till you can't breathe and then tears it out. We die a little too. But somehow we keep living. Every time we catch our reflection or see something we've done, even if it's just making a bed or laying a table, we find ourselves surprised that we are still capable of having any impact on the world. Death makes us feel like we're utterly powerless, like a ghost walking.'

They sat, both lost in thought. Then Lucy spoke 'They held on and held on, they fought, they never ever gave up on her, but eventually she was taken from them.'

'After Mia died Abe and Sarai must have grieved for ages because the next entry is over six months later. That part of the blog felt very different. They wanted to make some sense of what had happened and decided they needed to go on record to thank the medical staff. They made a film of the conversation they had with Mia's doctor.'

'She was younger than Sarai and Abe. She had such kind eyes, she never stopped looking at them when she was talking, but she seemed so, I don't know, compassionate. Abe started by saying they wanted to meet with her and thank her for everything she had done for Mia.'

She said something like *'That's kind of you, but I was just doing my job. I only wish I could have done more for Mia.'*

126

Sarai said she'd done loads, almost become one of the family. You could tell she thought they could never pay her back for all the help she'd given them. But the doctor just talked about how the hospital was there to serve people like them, and that knowing they'd done even something to help was what made her job worthwhile. You could tell she was really upset though. It wasn't just Mia she cared about, it was the whole family.

'And Sarai, oh she was great, she just couldn't keep quiet. She just kept on and on about how amazing this doctor had been and how she didn't have any choice but to protect and fight and care for Mia because she was her Mum. And she said not every doctor was like this one. This one was really special.

'And that was when the doctor said something really important. I've written it down. I'd like to get it into the story somehow.'

And here Lucy read from her notebook *'There's no one way to be a mother, or a father for that matter. There's no rule book. You just have to do your best. Parents have to find their way to know what that best is for them and their children just as much as we professionals do.'*

Anna reached out and took her niece's hand. 'That's so important for you to hang onto Lucy. Every Mum, every Dad does the best they can. You can't compare your Mum with Mia's parents. Your Mum didn't ask for the situation to be as it was when she got ill and you certainly didn't choose for her to get sick. When you're a parent everything changes, but nothing anyone says really prepares

127

you for how that makes you feel. One day I hope you'll be a Mum yourself and then you'll know what I mean. But just because you're a parent you don't suddenly become perfect.'

'Yes, but my Mum did something terrible. She chose to die. She thought she wasn't good enough and that her duty was to the Community. She wouldn't let me look after her. She was persuaded by the Duty Calls argument. Even though I was her child, and she knew I needed her, she gave up on herself not just because she was in pain but because she saw herself as being just ... a commodity. She thought she wasn't special, that she had no rights. Once she got ill she felt she had no value in the Community's eyes or hers.'

'But I loved her like Abe and Sarai loved Mia and they believed her life did have value, even when she was ill, for something more than just her ability to work or put something back, like I did with Mum. Mia didn't have to meet some 'standard' to be acceptable. And they thought they had a duty to fight to keep her. And Mia's illness actually inspired others to work and to try harder, to count their own blessings.'

Anna was struggling. 'The trouble is, love, life isn't black and white. What's right and what's wrong, what's fair and unfair, well, it just depends. Duty just means different things to different people, and at different times. It has to.'

'Yes, but love doesn't. Or it shouldn't do. Love's different.'

They sat in silence. Eventually Anna broke the peace.

'Did you speak to Jude about all this?'

'I did.'

'He doesn't know you're speaking to us as well does he? That has to be our secret. What did he have to say?'

Lucy looked deep into the fire.

'He listened, he was sympathetic of course. He's not a parent but he's not unfeeling. He said the same. Mum's situation was very different from Abe and Sarai's. In fact, he sort of said that their generation created Mum's situation. He said I should be proud of Mum's sacrifice. I just can't view her like that though and I don't want to think of Mum as a sacrifice. It's so unfair.'

The heavy silence continued to hang between them. A log slipped in the flames sending a shower of sparks upwards.

Finally Anna spoke. 'What are you going to do now?'

'Jude wants me to carry on. He's in a hurry for me to finish the story for the celebrations. He feels I can't allow what happened to Mum to cloud the message of Duty Calls for the Community. Maybe he's right. But I think he feels he's got me wrong.'

'What do you mean?'

Lucy shifted uneasily. 'I'm not sure. It was just something about the way he looked at me today. I think he's worried I might not be going to become quite as much of a Duty Calls convert as he'd hoped.'

Maybe it was her natural protectiveness, but Anna suddenly felt scared. What would Erin have said?

Finally she spoke. 'You know I love and believe in you, Lucy. But just be careful.'

Yesterday I was clever so I wanted to change the world, today I am wise so I want to change myself

Lucy found herself turning over and over again everything she was discovering about the past, her thoughts wandering when she was going about her daily chores. She tossed and turned at night, often falling into a fitful sleep and then waking unexpectedly, hot and sticky in the early hours, her mind snapping into gear even before she was fully conscious. Anna had probably put her finger on it. There were no answers, no rights or wrongs, just a whole tangle of history. The past was a muddle, a pile of twisted spaghetti in a bowl. Now it was too hard to find the start or end of any of the chains of events, unravel them and start again.

She felt better every time she spoke to Anna about it. 'Lucy, this isn't going to be easy. Think about what we all tend to do when we're faced with a problem that won't sort itself out, like a leaky roof. We can ignore it and hope it will go away. Or we make a start and tinker at the edges but give up when we realise just how hard it will be to fix. And very occasionally, and generally only when there's a flood we can't ignore, then we finally get ourselves into gear and get things sorted. Well, that's what I'm like with things that go wrong in my life anyway. It's not because I'm lazy, or stupid or don't care. I just get distracted. I don't see why we should expect anyone else, least of all our parents and grandparents, to have been any different, do you?'

'Nick's grandparents were born in the 1950s. They were probably too busy discovering sex and banning the bomb and experimenting with drugs when they were teenagers to worry too much about the future. And their parents had to deal with war and the fear of being overrun by Nazis. Those were real threats you couldn't ignore, death and destruction on your doorstep, in your own backyard. Every generation probably despairs of their children and thinks they are being irresponsible most of the time. Don't you think it's to be expected that it's sometimes only when stuff becomes desperate that people really do something? They might seem childish and irresponsible to us, but then they weren't living with the consequences the way we are.'

Lucy's nerves were visibly fraying. 'But Anna, these were Mums and Dads! Surely it was their DUTY to think ahead? I mean, Jude's not even a parent but he gets it, he thinks about this all the time! He says we need Duty Calls to protect the human race.'

'Of course parents get it,' Anna said. 'Most parents would take a bullet for their child. Without that the human race would have died out long ago. And I know this might sound strange but taking a bullet is, in a way, easier. You almost don't have to think. It's instinctive; you just go with your gut. The stuff you're looking at took years to happen. And it wasn't like they did nothing was it? They did try. Changing things takes huge amounts of energy you know. And you make loads of enemies along the way because lots of people wouldn't want to change because it suited them for things to stay as they were. You've found that out already.'

Lucy couldn't help it. She stamped her foot in passion. 'Oh Anna! You're so frustrating!' she shouted. 'You've got an answer for everything! I hate it when you won't just agree with me!'

Grabbing her coat, Lucy slammed out of the kitchen and made her way down to the beach. The sea always calmed her. She walked around for over an hour until her fingers were numb and it was too cold to stay out any longer and then she made her way wearily back. Anna said nothing, just poured hot water on some mint leaves and set the cup in front of her as she slumped at the kitchen table. The only sound was the clock ticking away in the corner.

'Sorry Anna.'

Her aunt held her tight. 'Don't say sorry. You've nothing to apologise for. It wouldn't be you if you didn't get passionate about all this.'

'I'm just so angry Anna. And tired, and muddled up.'

Her aunt came and sat down next to her at the table. 'I've been practicing a song on the ukulele,' she said. 'Would you like to hear it? Your Gramps taught me it.'

Lucy nodded. Anna took the instrument off the shelf behind the table and quickly tuned it. Then she started, very quietly, to sing. The tune was haunting and gentle. Lucy leaned across and let Anna hold her. After a few moments she sat up, wiped her nose on the back of her hand and smiled up at her aunt. Anna took her face in both hands and kissed her forehead lightly.

'You're so like your Mum sometimes, Lucy. She'd have been very proud of you. I remember your Grandma telling me once

132

about going with her parents on a holiday in an aeroplane. There used to be a safety announcement they all had to sit through, just as the flight was starting up, where the people that looked after you on the journey told you what to do if there was an emergency. It was ridiculous really. Even your Grandma as a little girl had worked out that if the plane went down and dived into the sea there was no hope!'

'But she told me there was this one thing they said that used to scare her a bit. They said that if you were a parent travelling with a child you had to fit your own oxygen mask before taking care of your children. That seemed all wrong to her. Surely she needed to be taken care of first, not her Mum! It took her a while to realise that if parents didn't look after their own needs then they'd be no help to their children.'

'In the long run, that's what your Mum was doing when she died, looking after you.'

Lucy thought about this for a while as she fell asleep. Maybe she was being hard on people in the past. Perhaps people had done things to try to save the world and couldn't have done anything about what she supposed they might have called acts of God.

But she still had this nagging feeling that it was all a bit like the safety announcements on the plane, or even the conferences and summits that had happened in the past. It was all a bit of a show. It made you feel something was being done, but really it was just smoke and mirrors.

On the sixth day

As she made her way, a week later, back through the familiar lanes now frosted and slippery with fallen leaves, Lucy knew with absolute certainty she would have to write two stories, one for Jude and one for herself. Jude expected evidence that illustrated his perception of previous generations: irresponsible and wasteful. But if she was to find peace and understanding for herself she would have to continue to explore Nick's blog. She knew he had created it for a reason.

She smiled to herself as she turned the key in the lock and made her way down to the crypt. Her grandfather had often said there was no peace for the wicked as he heaved himself up from his settee and set off to do whatever task he had set himself that day. She had no idea if she would find peace and she was fairly sure that in Jude's eyes she might be perceived as wicked if she didn't write the story the way he wanted her to. But she had to carry on. With a sigh, in part of anticipation and in part of sheer exhaustion, she turned on the laptop and set to work. Today's investigation was going to be for her, not Jude.

That night, once again, Lucy poured out her heart after supper to Anna.

'It's so complicated. One minute I'm baffled and angry, the next I'm just astonished by how kind people could be. '

Anna was busy making bread. She worked the dough steadily and expertly, turning and kneading it on the wooden table top worn to smoothness after many years of use. She loved to be busy. When she was finally happy with its condition she placed it in a bowl and left it to rise. Wiping her hands on a cloth she settled down in her favourite kitchen chair and closed her eyes for a moment. She marvelled at Lucy's intelligence and ability to think quickly, but she knew her own experience had given her insights and maybe even some wisdom over the years. The challenge, as ever, was to communicate in ways that would channel Lucy's passion without sounding patronising or critical. Not for the first time she longed for Erin.

'You've always been a free spirit, Lucy. You're not like me. I'm more of a follower. But you're a natural leader. You know how to make people listen when you talk about things that matter. You're clever. You can make something that's very complicated really easy for mere mortals like me to understand. You really don't recognise how good you are at stuff. You respect people because of who they are, not just their position. You are so generous in spirit and more forgiving of others than you are of yourself. I love you Lucy. It's no wonder Jude chose you. He of all people recognises your potential. He believes he can trust you. But maybe you need to be careful. If you challenge him, he'll smother you.'

Lucy smiled across at her aunt. 'Thanks Anna. I can't help it though. I feel sad, I feel angry. I'm really afraid to consider that Mum might have done the wrong thing in giving up on herself. I know it's hard, but I guess I feel lucky Jude chose me. I'm seeing things that happened over years all sort of telescoped together. That's helping me to make my own decisions about my past and what I want for my future.'

'We've said it before. Hindsight's a wonderful thing,' said Anna. 'It's as if you've got special glasses and you can see things people at the time missed. Sometimes it helps to look at a problem through the other end of the telescope. What seems huge is then very small, what seemed small can be seen really to have been huge.'

'The Time Capsule's working the way Nick and the others meant it to. It's transforming me. I feel like...I don't know....'

'A caterpillar becoming a butterfly?'

Lucy laughed. 'Exactly. Or an ugly little duckling turning into a beautiful swan!'

'And you know what it's doing to me listening to you telling the story?' asked Anna wistfully. 'It's making me realise that there's only so much people can do to change other people, or parents can do to protect their children. And that's hard to say when you're a Mum, I can tell you, when all you want to do is see your child happy and safe.'

Lucy unfolded a piece of paper. 'I needed to find out more about what was happening when Jude and Hope were born. I've wanted to understand whether by then some of the things that were happening to the planet had reached the point where they just couldn't be ignored anymore.'

'So today I asked the search engine: *What did fairness mean in 2035?* And I got such a shock. I found a webpage with a party political broadcast from something called the Fairness Party.'

'I vaguely remember my parents talking about them,' said Anna. 'But they were always a fringe group and by the time they got themselves established the world was probably in too much of a mess to be able to put their ideas into action.'

Lucy nodded. 'But there was something extraordinary about the broadcast. Something I never expected but I realised as soon as it began.'

'What?'

'Isaac, Jude's father, was the party leader! Nick and he must have had loads of arguments. They had the same goals but, if this broadcast is anything to go by, very different views about how to reach them. I had to write down every word because I was sure Jude would want to see what his father had said, if he hasn't done so already. Here, I'll read it to you.'

Party Political Broadcast on behalf of the Fairness Party: 2035. Delivered by Isaac Goodman

It's not fair. How often do we hear that? It's not fair that others have more than I have. It's not fair that I can't do what I want.

What's really not fair is that some of you, in spite of all your good fortune, waste your talents and think nothing of throwing away resources that you have. Or even worse, pursue your own selfish desires without any consideration of the impact of what you do, or

137

don't do, on others. What's fair about some people working hard to make the world a better and safer place while others simply mess with it, expecting the rest of us to pick up your pieces and put them back together again?

We have been given the most precious resource of all, our lives. And we have a duty to make something positive and constructive with those lives, not to waste them. Do what you want, yes, but only if you are not causing harm or detracting resources away that could meet the needs of others. That is only fair and just. Our individual actions cause ripples like a pebble being thrown into a pond. None of us has ever truly had, and now we can no longer afford, free will. We are all connected.

When elected, the Fairness Party will establish in every community a Duty Calls Centre where those who feel themselves no longer able to make a contribution to the community can be assessed and reassigned a more suitable task.

These reassignments will continue throughout the natural useful life span of an individual and, while in good health, could mean that we continue to make our contribution for many years. And, each time we're assessed, our worth is recalculated and reanalysed using a cost/benefit measure. And once cost outweighs benefit, well then Duty Calls!

Anna came back to the fireside and handed over a bowl of steaming soup.

'This is extraordinary, Lucy. This is what Jude's based his whole Duty Calls Centre idea on. Where has he learned all this from if not the Project?'

'I know. I'm supposing he must have heard his father and Nick talk about it all the time he was growing up. You should have seen the broadcast though, Anna. At the end there were these heroic images of old people walking into the sunset being cheered and waved off by adoring crowds. It was so different from the images in Nick's blog. He saw the sacrifice so differently.'

Anna shivered. 'It all sounds so manipulative.'

'That's exactly how it felt, clinical, controlled, unquestioning, obedient. And you know how I'd struggle with anything like that! Isaac kept describing how the world just could not afford to carry 'passengers'. He talked about the heroism of living and dying for your country and putting the greater good before your own personal safety or that of your family.'

'Some of that does sound heroic,' said Anna. 'It's ideology. It's the kind of stuff that justified mothers, wives and daughters sacrificing their sons, husbands and fathers in wars to save the world.'

'I know. These ideas must have lodged in Jude's memory from when he was young. They 'make sense' now because of the scarcity of our resources.'

Anna murmured: *'Ask not what your country can do for you, ask rather what you can do for your country.'*

Lucy looked down at her hands and folding her arms tightly around her body she rocked gently in the chair.

'All the time I've been working with the Time Capsule I've been struck by how quickly all the really important changes happened. And you know what that's made me think? How quick it would seem looking back that my life and your life and Seb's life would cease to be viewed as 'useful' and it would be our turn, just like it was Mum's. I mean, this was only 80 years ago. Think about how much changed in Grandpa's life. Things are always closer than we think.'

'Jude talks so much about duty, but he doesn't talk about how we feel towards each other. Sure, I wouldn't say I *deserve* to be cared for. But I think I agree with Nick. I believe all of us have rights to live, to make our own choices about what we do with our lives. I want to live in a world that goes beyond logic and duty and has room for love. And if we can't have that world I'm not sure I want to live any more.'

Anna hated seeing her struggle like this. Erin would have been so proud of her.

'I can remember my parents having these discussions and impressing on me that I mattered, that I needed to stay well, that I should always work hard and do my best for others, but that no one could save the world, the most important thing was to save yourself,' said Anna. 'They would describe it as pragmatism, picking your fights, being realistic.'

'I can see it now,' said Lucy. They were trying to be good parents too. They wanted to make sure that you focused your energy, your resources on your survival. And they succeeded. Who's to say they weren't good parents? Their way saved your life and Mum's, like Isaac's way saved Jude. Now I think I need to find out if Nick's way saved Hope.'

On the seventh day

It was Lucy's final day at the Time Capsule. She knew exactly what she had to do. Nick had had a child, Hope, born in 2035, the same year as Jude. He had kept a video diary of her life much as his parents had done of his and Mia's.

By now Lucy had abandoned all pretence of trying to complete the story Jude wanted her to tell. She accessed the diary and focused like she had never focused before. She wanted to make sure she missed no detail, that she scrutinised the evidence with a magnifying glass. She needed to look, she needed to see and, more than anything else, she needed to understand.

Almost immediately she was struck as she watched Hope's story unfold on screen by the values and beliefs with which she had grown up. They were very different from the ones Jude had experienced. Every so often a young Jude appeared in the videos, always more hesitant and awkward than Hope, but there was an easy familiarity between them as cousins. It reminded her of herself and Seb.

In one scene Hope took the camera from her father and showed the unseen 'audience' round her room. It was full of her. Pictures she'd drawn were placed in bright disarray on a pin board, clothes thrown haphazardly over a wicker chair, some photographs propped up on the windowsill. One of the very few elements that appeared to have been placed neatly was a framed poster hanging on the wall at the foot of Hope's bed. It spoke of the wisdom of learning to play fair and clear up your own mess in the world. Lucy knew this was telling her something she needed to pay attention to. So she did just what the words of the poster urged her to do. She looked. And what she saw was that Hope lived in a family that held hands and stuck together.

When Hope's grandparents, Abe and Sarai fell ill, for example, and were unable to work she saw them being cared for by the whole family. They did less work outside the home in order to focus on looking after them.

She observed how Nick would do anything to protect his daughter but that he pushed her to think for herself. She became before her eyes just like him, strong and compassionate, but also impatient and challenging. Lucy liked to think she and Hope might have been friends.

'Nick was teaching Hope how to use a camera,' she told Anna that night. 'He wanted her to learn how to chronicle stories the way he'd seen his Mum doing for their family. And she clearly has a rare gift for doing it. The video diary she kept got better each week.'

'There was one scene where someone, probably Sarai, is filming Nick, Hope and Jude snuggled up on the sofa one Christmas watching what Nick describes as a 'classic'. It was that old film Gramps used to tell us he watched when he was a child, do you remember? *Avatar*. There's a lovely moment where both of them giggle as Nick turns to them at the end, and says one of the lines of

Jake, who's the main character. He says *'I see you, Hope. I see you Jude.'*

'Later there's a part of the blog that Hope films herself. You see her settle her father down in front of the camera and set the whole thing up as if it's an interview.

Lucy had enjoyed watching this scene.

'So *Mr Grigori, why, in your opinion, is Avatar such a classic?'*

Playing to the camera, Nick had hammed up his role. *'Well Hope, I'm glad you've asked me that. Avatar is indeed a great film. In it we see how the 'civilised humans' turn out to be primitive, jaded and increasingly greedy, cynical, and brutal. These are traits only amplified by their machinery. On the other hand the 'monkey aliens', the Na'vi, emerge as noble, kind, wise, sensitive and humane. We, along with the Avatar hero, Jake, are now faced with an uncomfortable yet irresistible choice between two races and two world views. It is inevitable that the audience, like Jake, will find that the Na'vi's culture was really the more civilized of the two, exemplifying qualities of kindness, gratitude, regard for the elder, self-sacrifice, respect for all life and ultimately humble dependence on a higher intelligence behind Nature.'*

'Do you think it's an important film for people to see?'

'Oh yes, Hope I really do. I would urge every man, woman and child on the planet to see the film and wake up to its message by making the right choice between commercial materialism, which is

steamrolling our soul and consciousness, and reconnection with all life as the only promise of survival for humanity.'

'There's a lot of destruction in the film. Mr Grigori, do you think ultimately it is a film that gives us any hope?'

'Absolutely. With the union of humans and aliens depicted in the film comes a feeling that something better exists in the universe: the respect for life. The Na'vi represent the better aspects of human nature, and the human characters in the film demonstrate the more destructive aspects of human nature.'

'I believe the director, James Cameron, really wanted us to think about how we treat the world's natural environment. I think he felt we were going to experience a lot of pain and heartache if we didn't acknowledge our stewardship responsibilities to Nature, and I think he's right. There's a lot in the film that challenges our attitude that somehow we are entitled to use up resources.'

'Avatar is saying our attitudes about indigenous people and our entitlement about what is rightfully theirs is the same sense of entitlement that lets us bulldoze a forest and not blink an eye. It's just human nature that if we can take something, we will. And sometimes we do that in a very naked and imperialistic way, and other times we do it in a very sophisticated way with lots of rationalization. But it's basically the same thing that motivates us. A sense of entitlement. And we can't just go on in this unsustainable way, just taking what we want and not giving back. The film's about the brutality of man, who shamelessly takes what isn't his, not thinking about the consequences in the longer term.'

As Lucy described the scene Anna realised she knew about this film too. Her parents' first date had been going to their local cinema to see *Avatar* when it appeared as part of a series of classic movies. Her mother had fallen a little bit in love with Jake, the hero of the film. She had smiled to herself when she had told Anna and Erin the story remembering how their father had quoted the main line from the film at the end of the evening. *'I see you Christina,'* he had smiled as he had kissed her, at first gently just touching his lips to hers but with increasing warmth and longing, after he had walked her home on a balmy June evening a lifetime ago.

When the transmissions in the Time Capsule came to an end Lucy's last sight of Hope was of a passionate fifteen year old reflecting her father's values and trying to do what she could to save the planet. She had learned that Nick had taught her all he could about the areas of land that were most likely to survive the impact of global warming. She could see that the family would have been easily characterised as 'alternative', even deluded.

The video diary revealed that Nick and Hope's relationship was very close but did not always run smoothly. In one extract towards its ending they were communicating via Skype:

Nick: Hi lovely girl, what's occurring?

Hope: Hi Dad. All good. How's you?

Nick: Good thanks. Busy with work stuff, should be home about 7ish. I'll look over that history course work with you then if you like. Due in tomorrow isn't it?

Nick: Or have I got that wrong?

Nick: Is it due in tomorrow? You know that essay you have to do?

Nick: Hope?

Nick: Is it due in tomorrow, that essay?

Nick: Hope, are you there?

Nick: Have you done that essay? I'll check it over with you tonight.

Hope: I'm out tonight.

Nick: Have you done the essay?

Hope: No Dad, I've not done the fizzing essay. And I'm going out tonight to the rally.

Nick: Why?

Hope: You know why.

Nick: Try explaining it to me.

Hope: Dad, you know the rally's more important than a bloody essay.

Nick: Because...?

Hope: Because the rally's about saving the planet and the essay's about people that are already dead. That's why. I'm going to the rally. I don't give a toss about the essay.

Nick: The essay that counts towards your grades? The essay that'll help you get to university? You don't care about that?

Hope: No. I don't. Not right now, no. I care about the rally and I care about being with everyone else and actually doing something for once instead of going along with all this 'what you going to do with your future' crap. There's not going to be any bloody future at this rate if we don't do something to make people wake up and listen.

Nick: You have to do the essay.

Hope: You're not listening to me Dad. Which is a joke given everything you're always going on about. Bet you'll be at the bloody rally.

Nick: I don't have an essay to hand in tomorrow. I've already got my grades, gone to university, got a job. You haven't.

Nick: Have you even started the essay?

Hope: Yes.

Nick: How much have you done?

Nick: Have you done a plan?

Hope: Sort of.

Nick: Sort of?

Hope: There's stuff in my jotter.

Nick: In your jotter?

Nick: What's the stuff in your jotter?

Nick: Notes?

Hope: Yeah, notes.

Nick: What you doing this afternoon?

Hope: I'm on study leave. Going to help Mum make posters for the rally.

Nick: I'll speak to her. Do the essay.

Lucy's last sighting of Hope was against the backdrop of some of the worst ravages of climate change and global pandemics sweeping through towns and cities. Nick and the family were packing up their home and gathering the last of their friends and family together to begin a trek north.

She remembered something her grandmother used to quote to her often. *'If there is one thing that I have learnt about life, it goes on.'*

She wanted so much to believe that was true, but had a real sense of foreboding as she watched the Grigoris being filmed disappearing northwards. They presented as a ramshackle group, old and young, Nick supporting his mother, Sarai, who looked very frail. They were very unlike the Community. Their determination to take with them anyone, even without screening for disease or their ability to 'put back' appeared, to Lucy's eyes, to spell inevitable disaster for them all.

Lucy was really torn in her conversation that night with Anna.

'I love Nick because he must have been a great Dad to have. But he almost certainly didn't protect Hope from death. Isaac had an approach that was very different. That's probably what saved Jude. And Gramps and Grandma, well they saved their own. You and Mum did survive and that's the only reason me and Seb are here. And then there's Mum, and I don't know what to think about Mum anymore.'

Anna knelt beside her niece and wrapped her arms around her, holding her tight

'She did what she did because she loved you. She had no choice.'

Lucy could hardly speak. She rocked back and forth in the chair by the fireside.

'She did have a choice. There's always a choice. She was *my* Mum.'

She pushed away from Anna and with an enormous effort pulled herself back up in the chair and looked deep into her aunt's eyes. Taking a huge breath she whispered:

'Was she a good Mum or the worst one ever? I just don't know any more. But I miss her. Why couldn't I save her?'

And then she turned into the chair, shutting Anna out. Her aunt sat silently, hands resting in her lap, face filled with concern, sensing the pain Lucy must be feeling. She had no idea where this would end.

The Message

That night Lucy tossed and turned until the early hours. The next day, to her complete surprise, she was summoned by Jude. His manner was businesslike and brusque.

'I have turned our recent conversations over in my mind, Lucy, and it is, with regret, that I am going to have to end your work on the Project.'

'What? Why?'

'I have made an error of judgement. You do not have the necessary wisdom or experience needed to write the Community's story. I want you to go back to the laptop tomorrow, pull together everything you have done so far and leave the work in a fit condition for someone else that I will select to take over from you and finish the task.'

Lucy knew she had no choice but to obey. She was incandescent with rage. Who did he think he was?

'I won't go quietly,' she said to Anna and Seb that night.

At first light Lucy went directly to Jude's house and collected the key for the crypt. She said nothing about her intentions. But she knew exactly what she had to do.

Using the search engine she went back to Nick's *20/20 Vision* speech. She marvelled at the extent to which it powerfully and eloquently spelt out why all human life had value in itself. Human beings were not commodities. She revelled in the way Nick talked about the need not to wait passively but to take action. The reminder that there was no such thing as a standard for human beings to reach in order to earn acceptability brought a lump to her throat.

Lucy pounded at the keys without pausing for more than an hour, creating and saving a document which she called 'Our Story.' Then, even though she knew the address that appeared at the end of the broadcast was long defunct, she opened it up, clicked on 'new message', attached the document, wrote a covering note, and before she could stop to think, pressed 'Send.'

To: Hope Grigori

I have seen your father's *20/20 Vision*. It is about to come to pass and no matter what I do any more, I can't stop it. Please, if you are still out there, it is far too late for me, but I have to believe it is not too late for my Community. I beg you to read our story and help us.

Lucy Daniel

Our Story: by Lucy Daniel

It is 2099. We are nearly at the end of the 21st century. I live in a small Community. Our home is a rocky island you can only get to by boat or by crossing a causeway at low tide. We work together to survive. But we all have memories of our past.

This is our story.

I have been able to see information on a data storage device that has been downloaded onto a laptop hidden in the crypt of a church in my Community. The device is a Time Capsule, with information dating back to the 20th century, around the time my great grandparents were alive. The data comes from something called the World Wide Web. That was a good name for it, because it captured information from across the whole world.

The device was produced by a Project called the *20/20 Vision* that ran, on and off, for over 20 years until 2050. I only found out about it when I was given this opportunity. The aim of that Project was to educate and to warn people like me and the rest of the Community. It was run by a group of academics and eco warriors who left a trail they wanted people like us to follow.

They didn't know it, but they left it for me.

They had a story to tell. Though it was too late for them, they believed in what that story would teach others. So they created this archive. What it contains was not a secret back then. The *20/20 Vision* team felt no one was looking or paying attention to the warning signs of what was happening in the world. Or if they were, they believed people: individuals, governments and authorities were not doing enough about what those signs meant for the planet. They created the archive so those to come could learn from the past.

I was born in 2082. I have only ever known the world as it is now. It is a world where all of the basic resources we need to survive are incredibly scarce.

For this story I am also drawing on the tales I was brought up on. The stories I was told by my Mum and my Dad, my grandparents, my great grandparents. They said they loved and cared for me. So I am trying to understand why they allowed these things to happen.

This is what I know.

Between 2040 and 2090 there were a whole range of natural and manmade disasters in the world. These led to the loss of many of the resources my grandparents would have taken for granted. Some of those disasters had been predicted, some not. But they took place so quickly and in such close succession that the human race found it impossible to cope with their impact.

As a consequence our lives today are changed out of all recognition.

When it was evident that it was too late to stop the devastation, governments finally started to take action together for the good of what might be left of the planet. One of the most significant things they did was to shut down all nuclear reactors and weaponry. That prevented what could otherwise have happened, a final potential horror: leakage from unmaintained power stations and radioactive contamination.

In spite of frantic last minute attempts to make things better, the human race really did seem about to be extinguished. People had to find ever changing ways to survive as conditions rapidly deteriorated. Eventually some degree of stability began to develop in parts of the world where life was still possible. Northern Europe was one of the last outposts of the planet capable of sustaining life.

Small settlements began to spring up where we could work closely together to grow food and farm. People have in some instances moved huge distances in order to settle in a place where they feel they may have some chance of survival. We have no way of knowing how many of these exist or where they are. There is a growing suspicion in my Community that everyone else is either dead or on the verge of extinction. Although there is an interest in what might be happening elsewhere, those of us that survive focus on just staying alive.

My Community

My story is set in a Community of around 500 that has been gradually establishing. We live in small settlements in cottages and farmhouses, dotted around the island. Our population was at first added to as refugees trickled in from across the country and sometimes by boat from mainland Europe.

Each new arrival that could contribute to the Community is regarded as very precious, a commodity for sustaining food production and contributing to the gene pool. However, before accepting them we have to know that their 'cost' as an individual will be outweighed by their 'benefit'. We are vulnerable to diseases. Refugees are quarantined before being allowed to join the Community.

There is a certain amount of pride in knowing that we are part of a tiny population that has survived. But this pride is tempered by fear of extinction. A feeling of responsibility at being potentially some of the few members of the human race that have managed to remain alive runs through everything we do. In many ways we in the Community are not dissimilar from explorers or a landing party setting up a new existence in a previously undiscovered world. There are too few of us to be complacent.

For us, all resource is precious. For some, including our Chief Steward who has responsibility for us all, the needs of the Community as a whole outweigh the needs of the individual. He believes we cannot afford to lose focus or be sentimental and that our duty is to any future we can create together, whatever the cost. Even if that cost includes sacrificing the lives of those we hold most dear because the cost of maintaining their life outweighs the benefits they can bring, we must pay that price. That is what he says our duty calls us to do.

This task was about me helping all of us as a Community to commit to his Duty Calls approach. But this is not what *20/20 Vision* has taught me. Instead it has taught me this:

Every one of us has the gift of life.

A leader's first duty is to create the conditions to protect everyone in a Community

Leaders in the past failed in this most basic of responsibilities

But we have the chance to start again.

I want a Community where

We are not judged for what we can or cannot do, but loved as individuals

All our resources are shared fairly so no one is left behind

My right to live or to die lies with no one but myself

This is the Community I choose

The night of October 31st 2099

'I am going to find a way to leave the Community.'

Lucy was standing, panting and breathless, in the doorway of Anna's cottage. Once she had sent her message and the story she had run all the way back from the church without stopping.

'Leave?' said Anna. 'You can't do that.'

'Oh I can, and I will. I can't stop Jude, but I won't submit to Duty Calls. I'm not Mum.'

Seb stood up. 'I'm coming with you.'

'What? You are not young man. You're staying right where you are.'

'Mum, Lucy's right, and I'm not a child any more, you can't tell me what to do. I hate Duty Calls every bit as much as she does. Haven't you always taught me to listen to my conscience, do the right thing? Well, that's what I'm doing. I can't go along with this any longer. We've got to find a way to take back control. I want to be with Lucy.'

'You haven't thought this through. Where will you go? Who will take care of you?'

Lucy took Anna's hands in hers and spoke with real intensity. 'Let's not make up problems that might not even be there. I'm not going to let Jude make the decisions about how I live, or how I die. Seb, you know I love you, but it's got to be your choice. It will mean leaving everything and everyone, but at least we'll be free.'

This was it, she thought as she made her way through the village. This was finally it.

It was a foul night. The wind lashed the rain into her face like glass splinters and she wrapped her scarf round her mouth and nose so only her eyes were visible peering over the top into the darkness. She had to lean forward into the bombardment and press against it until eventually she half ran, half fell into Jude's door, rattling the knocker with as much strength as she could muster. As it swung open she tumbled inside and, barely keeping her feet, she stood catching her breath as he battled to close and bolt the door behind her. Only then did the candles stop their sputtering but the sound of the crackling and spitting of the fire still competed with the howling gale outside and the rattling and creaking of the very bones of the cottage.

She blurted it out. 'We're leaving Jude,' she said, not bothering with any of the usual pleasantries. 'Seb and me. We're going at first light. We're not taking resources with us, look,' and here she indicated Lela who was shaking off as much of the rain as she could from her sodden coat and making her way straight to the fireside to warm herself. 'Even though it breaks my heart to do it, I'm leaving you Lela. She still has a job to do here. We're just taking responsibility for our own lives and our own deaths. We're not hurting anyone else by going.'

She thought she saw an expression of something she could not place: fear, menace, hate, momentarily flicker across Jude's face, but it was gone before she could be sure it had even existed. But she shivered involuntarily. It was if someone had walked over her grave. Although he spoke levelly, she could tell from his clenched hands that Jude was furious.

'Maybe you're hurting no one in the short term, Lucy, but if you go this sets a precedent. If everyone did what you propose then the Community would fail and, ultimately humanity would be eradicated. What you are proposing is not fair to the Community. How many times must I say this? We cannot afford personal rights and personal freedoms. We are only strong together.'

'I don't want to be strong together! I want to be weak if I have to be, I want to be compassionate to someone I care about if I want to be. I'd rather have a kind heart than a so called wise head. Finally I get it, Jude. Duty Calls is nothing more than a cover up for a way of controlling and dominating us all. I don't care what you say, you can't stop us. We're leaving.'

And with that, Lucy flung the key to the crypt on the floor, wrenched open the door and ran, as fast as she could, tears and rain running in equal measure down her face.

Seb was watching at the window and saw Lucy as she battled against the storm and into her cottage. There was no sign of Lela so he guessed Jude must have taken her. He wondered about going through to see Lucy straight away but changed his mind. Who knows how Jude had taken the news and it was probably as well to give her some time to herself.

Anna was sitting sewing by the fireside. Her eyes rested on her son as he went about his chores for the last time. She was overwhelmed with emotions and so proud of him. Somehow through all of this he had found his purpose, his moral compass. There was so much of children that parents did not know about, that they kept hidden, why? To stop you from interfering, to protect you, to stop them having to reveal the depths of their own uncertainties about who they were? But she sensed there was something different about Seb tonight. He knew what he wanted. Finally he knew who he was.

The room was quiet and cosy. Seb knelt at Anna's feet and rested his head in her lap. 'I'm ready now, Mum.'

She put down her sewing and stroked his soft dark curls. 'I know son.'

They hugged each other tightly for what felt like an age. When they let each other go Anna said simply 'Time for bed. Big day ahead tomorrow.'

'I think I'll just check Lucy's alright before I turn in. I love her you know, Mum. We just want to be together.'

'I know you do. You always have done. Now don't wake me when you come back, I'm going to bed. I'll see you in the morning.'

And with that she gave him one last hug, went through to her bedroom and closed the door.

Seb pulled on his jacket and, bracing himself to meet the howling wind, stepped outside into the darkness. Keeping close to the wall he started the short journey across the yard to his cousin's. But he had barely gone a few steps when suddenly he was grabbed from behind and an arm was pulled tightly round his throat. He struggled but a cloth was clamped hard across his mouth filled with pungent odour. Almost instantly he swooned, collapsing like a felled tree. It was over in seconds.

Jude pulled the body into the shadows and laid it as far out of the wind and rain as he could. He glanced furtively about him. His eyes had become accustomed to the darkness and, like a nocturnal predator, he had an ability to see when everyone else was blind. But the weather was foul and there was no one else who was foolish enough to have ventured out. Moving stealthily across to Lucy's cottage he managed to peer through a chink and watched intently as she undressed and climbed into bed. She blew out the candle and the cottage was suddenly in darkness.

He knew he had to wait until he could be sure she was asleep. Pressed against the wall of the hen house he huddled in the lee of the wind, turning over and over in his mind the details of the plan he had rapidly devised and the rationale behind it. He was shaking, as much with excitement as with cold. Glancing about him he took in the scene: the black outlines of trees bending and dancing like wild witches in the howling gale, the full moon with dark clouds scudding across it so it only emerged momentarily and then was hidden again. What was it he felt: excitement, fear, determination? Yes, it was all of those. But most of all, he felt alive.

After what he judged was a long enough period of time he crept to Lucy's door and painstakingly and warily lifted the latch, stopping and adjusting his hold on it at every sound. He opened it just wide enough to slip in and then just as carefully closed it behind him.

He stood, almost holding his breath and listened. There was silence apart from the steady breathing coming from the figure he sensed rather than saw sleeping in the bed. No Lela of course. She was safely tied up back in his house. How fortunate that they had decided to give her to him just when he needed her out of the way. He waited till his eyes had grown accustomed to the darkness and then made his way by the light of the last embers of the fire to the sofa, collected the largest cushion he could find and tiptoed over to where Lucy was lying, fast asleep.

He looked down at her and for a brief moment allowed himself to let his eyes roam over her sleeping body. Her hair tumbled round her face, the creamy white flesh of her neck and upper breast exposed and vulnerable. She looked peaceful and childlike. This was how he liked her.

With one swift movement he pounced. Lucy's eyes opened and she tried to scream, but he was straddling her, pressing the cushion down hard over her mouth and nose, his whole weight pinning her back into the bed. She fought and struggled, but she was overwhelmed. Just before the end her eyes locked on Jude's and went still. He saw something in that look he did not understand. It felt like defiance. In spite of himself, he flinched.

When it was over, Jude clambered off her body and quickly made his way back outside. He returned slowly, staggering and panting under Seb's weight. He lowered him as carefully as he could onto the bed next to Lucy and again picked up the cushion. It was much easier this time.

Making sure that the door was closed and with another quick glance around the yard to check no one was watching, Jude rapidly stripped both the bodies, tossing the clothes randomly to the floor as if they had been removed in a frenzied passion. Once both bodies were naked, he curled them together, placing Seb's hand on Lucy's breasts cradling her from behind, pressing him tightly around her. He took the hemlock from his pocket and rubbed it on their lips, then put the remainder into two drinking bowls which he had placed on either side of them.

When he had set the scene he stood back and surveyed his handiwork. Was it convincing enough? He knew it had to be perfect, in every particular.

He allowed his eyes to relish the scene, delighting in every detail of the young exposed flesh before him. And then he was gone.

One month later

Anna knew she would never recover from the loss. The pain would always be there. The best she could hope for was that one day time would anaesthetise the hurt and her grief would deaden.

She had woken early and gone straight to Lucy's the moment she had realised Seb was not at home. Call it a mother's intuition, but as soon as she had opened her eyes she had a feeling something was wrong.

She had not though expected just how wrong. Pulling back the blanket on Lucy's bed she had revealed two ice cold bodies, limbs entwined, lips tinged blue, a musty smell hanging over them. She had stared in disbelief, her mind racing, trying to piece together events as they must have happened. She saw the scattered clothes, the empty drinking vessels once filled with poison, the tenderness of their embrace revealing just how much they must have longed to be together.

'Star crossed lovers,' said Jude later that evening. 'Romeo and Juliet.'

Wrung out with crying, Anna searched her heart for something that would help it all to make sense.

'I just never saw it coming,' she whispered. 'I mean, I knew they were both passionate and over wrought, that they both wanted to take control of their destiny, that they loved each other dearly. But I hadn't realised, I never thought it was like this. And it's strange to say now, but I sometimes used to wonder if Seb would grow to be a man that wanted a woman,' she faltered. 'It was nothing he said, just a feeling I had.'

Jude studied her kindly. 'Sadly now we will never know, Anna. These two young people's passion was unlawful. Their genetic closeness meant it could never have been permitted. They would have known that.'

It was the night before their funerals that Jude had taken her to the crypt and shown her Lucy's final saved document. She had read the whole story slowly, and wept.

'She broke her promise to you, Jude,' she said when she had finally finished. She told me and Seb all about the laptop and the Project but I never guessed it would end like this. If I'd read this in time then maybe I would have been able to make them see sense and stop them. I promised Erin I'd protect her.'

'You must not blame yourself,' Jude said with something like tenderness. 'Young people can be so passionate. Their hearts rule their heads. If anyone is at fault, it is me.'

Anna protested but he would not be comforted.

'Seb and Lucy were so young. I asked too much of them. They could not be expected to control their emotions in the way that we, as their elders, know is necessary. The value of doing our duty is something we can learn only with age. I misjudged that. All that matters or makes sense now is that we ensure the Community survives, you and I. That survival will be Lucy's legacy. I want this to be presented as her story, not mine, in a way that, if only I could have made her see, she would have understood. I need you to help me, Anna. Will you take over Lucy's work for me and for her?'

Anna hesitated. Lucy had hated Duty Calls, but not the *20/20 Vision.* Accessing it had opened her eyes in a way that had changed her irreversibly. Anna knew she had to grasp this opportunity to see the archive for herself. It was her chance to follow in Lucy's footsteps. She would have to be careful, but she could never forgive herself if she did not at least try to understand why this had happened and make some sense of it all.

So it was that one cold day early in December Anna found herself in the same crypt, sat at the same laptop and putting her hands on the same arms of the chair as Lucy had done only a few weeks before. She closed her eyes and trying to be mindful of the moment, searched for a way to be open and to connect with her niece.

'Oh Lucy,' she breathed finally. 'May you know peace, at last.'

She tried to focus on the screen. As she was about to click on the folder that she guessed contained the document Lucy had almost finished, the machine pinged.

Puzzled, Anna lifted the laptop from the table, looking underneath and behind it. She could see nothing, no bell, no other device. But she did notice something odd. There were wires running from the back of the laptop down behind the table and disappearing through a hole in the wall. Crouching down she tried to see where they went, but the wall was too thick. Had Lucy ever mentioned this? Or Jude? They each must have known these wires were there.

Going back to the screen Anna noticed there was an icon flashing. She moved the cursor over it, clicked and read Lucy's message to Hope. It reminded her of something she had once done as a child on holiday. She had wanted to see if it was possible to communicate with someone you could not see and simply had to trust might be there.

'It's a message in a bottle,' she murmured.

Then she sprang to her feet so suddenly, she tipped over the chair. It went crashing to the floor. Space had been Lucy's ocean. The message had been a cry, a prayer cast, apparently, into a void.

But it had been 'liked'.

With trembling fingers, Anna replaced the chair. She could not believe her eyes. Barely able to breathe, she hovered the cursor over the icon and clicked. Four words and a picture appeared.

'I see you Lucy.'

In front of Anna was an image of a woman from the past, who had responded to a message sent from a desperate teenager into the future. She stared at the face on the screen. She had no idea how it could be possible, or what it meant, but with absolute certainty she knew who this woman had to be.

It was Hope.

The Secret

'When the hell were you going to tell us?'

Face contorted with anger, Anna pushed past Jude and forced her way across the threshold of the cottage the instant he responded to the sound of her fists pounding on his door. Chest heaving with the effort of running as fast as she could from the church, she stood, red faced, fists clenched, eyes flashing.

'Anna, what are you talking about? Tell you what?'

'About Hope of course! That she's out there! That we're not the only ones left!'

Jude went white and dropped like a stone into a chair.

'What do you mean?'

'Don't give me that, I know everything! She's tried to contact Lucy and when I messaged her back she thought it was you.'

Terror flashed across the Chief Steward's face. Anna lunged at him and he cringed over the table wrapping his arms above his head to protect himself as she rained blows down onto him.

'You had no right to keep this from us,' she screamed. 'They would never have killed themselves if they'd known.'

She flung herself across the room and stood, shoulders shaking. Jude remained where he was, still, head and face hidden under the sleeves of his robe. As her sobbing diminished he slowly raised his head.

'Anna, you have to believe me, I did everything for the best.'

She wrenched open the door and fled.

***   ***   ***   ***

He found her huddled on some rocks down by the sea. She was shivering in the cold, her finger ends numb, nose running, face streaked with tears. Pausing, he glanced quickly around and then took up a position alongside her, just far enough away to avoid any flaying fists but close enough for her to hear him above the sound of the incoming tide.

'I was going to tell you, I was going to tell you all. I never thought this would happen Anna. And that's the truth.'

She continued to look straight ahead.

'Nothing you say is going to bring them back though, is it?'

'No, it's not.'

They stayed till there was no feeling left in any part of their limbs and when they tried to stand they half stumbled, half fell and had to cling together as they picked their way back from the shoreline. Slowly they made their way to Anna's cottage. Once inside, Jude half carried her into a chair, wrapped a blanket round her shoulders and quickly made up the fire. As the room started to warm he handed her a steaming mug and they both huddled as near to the heat as they could, the flames licking round the branches and sending dancing shadows onto the walls.

'So, what do you know?'

There was a long pause.

'It was Lucy,' she said 'She sent Hope a message.'

'I don't understand.'

'Nor do I. She must have been desperate.'

'How did she know Hope was out there?

'I don't think she did. I think she just took a chance. And it paid off.'

Silence descended again, only broken by the crackling of the fire.

'Why did you keep this a secret, Jude? Where is Hope?'

Jude was leaning forward in his chair. He stared into the fire as he spoke.

'She's coming to us.'

'What? Coming here? To the Community? When? How?

'On New Year's Eve. To the Ceremony. With her people.'

'That's what Lucy's story was to be used for? A welcoming ceremony?'

'Yes, Anna, that's what Lucy's story is for.'

'Why didn't you tell her?'

'Why do you think? You said yourself she couldn't keep quiet about the laptop. Do you honestly think she could have kept this to herself? She wasn't ready to be told.'

'Told what, exactly?'

'That Hope is alive, that she has a Community of her own, that they want to join with us.'

Anna shook her head. 'I don't believe you. It's not possible.'

Jude sighed. 'It was the *20/20 Vision* Project team. They didn't just produce the archive. They also set up a network of transmitters and receivers that would allow survivors to communicate. They identified a few key locations where communities had the best chance of establishing themselves. It was very basic, unsophisticated technology, but it worked.

Anna slowly processed the information.

'So, you mean there could be more communities out there, not just Hope's?'

'Not could be. There are. She's been in touch with some of them.'

Anna was stunned.

'But why aren't we talking to them then? Why aren't we getting together?'

Jude was still staring into the fire.

'It's too risky, Anna. We don't know what those communities are like.'

'What do you mean? They'll be like us won't they?'

Jude turned to her.

'Why should they be?'

Their eyes locked. Slowly understanding was dawning on her.

'It's my duty to protect this Community. I tried to impress that on Lucy, but she wouldn't listen.'

'But she didn't know all this! You should have trusted her. She wasn't a child.'

'And do you think that she'd have gone along with my plans if she had known? I couldn't be certain. It was too big a risk. And I was *absolutely convinced* that Duty Calls is the only way to protect ourselves long term. I still am.'

'Why?'

'Because my first duty to you as your leader is to make sure our Community survives. Hope was brought up with very different ideas from me. I tried to get Lucy to understand that. She sees all people as having needs that communities should meet. To Hope, there are no 'standards' people have to reach, no 'passengers.' Everyone belongs by right. And her Community reflects that.'

'So?'

'So, her Community is failing. Of course it is. You cannot have a community that looks after everyone equally when resources are limited. Increasingly those that can work cannot produce enough to support those that cannot. And, to make matters worse, in Hope's Community their children, specifically their baby girls, are not surviving but dying in their early years, which means they have fewer women with child bearing capabilities available. Many baby girls are simply dying at birth. They don't know why this is happening, but it's become an increasing pattern.'

'So that's why they want to join with us?'

'Exactly. We have the reproductive capabilities that they lack. But we will have to be cautious. They bring with them strong men who will give us much needed labour at least. They will allow more of our young women to have time away from manual work and create the capacity for them to care for our children. However, we cannot assume that the genetic material of these young men is intact. We will have to test that.'

Jude, ever the pragmatist, thought Anna. She could not bear to listen to any more. She felt suddenly exhausted and closed her eyes. He got to his feet.

'This has been a huge amount for you to take in Anna. It is no wonder you are tired. I will leave you now and we will talk further in the morning when you are rested.'

Without opening her eyes she nodded and he made to leave, pausing only at the door to look back at her for a few moments before he slipped away.

Integration

She struggled with her thoughts all night, finally falling into a fitful sleep shortly before dawn. Her arm cradled Lela who had long since abandoned her basket and now regularly slept on Anna's bed, a warm and comforting presence.

As soon as she awoke she went to Jude. He had guessed she would be back early and he was up and about waiting for her.

'So, what happens now?'

Jude studied Anna's face carefully before replying, then appeared to make up his mind. 'I am going to trust you with information Anna, on one condition. You must tell no one what I am about to share.'

'Hope and around 300 of her Community are on their way here right now. They have a long journey, but all being well they will arrive in time for New Year. Hope and I have been planning this for some time, ever since I first made contact with her over a year ago.'

'You've known about Hope for a year?'

'Yes, ever since you failed to bring back the two children safely from the lighthouse.' He paused and looked at her closely and for a moment she wondered if he knew about Sam's grave after all. 'That was a turning point for me. It was an indication of how little chance there was of any other refugees reaching us. I believed we were, still are, highly vulnerable and I was desperate. The best chance we had it seemed was for me to use the laptop and send out messages into the ether, much as Lucy did, and trust that someone, somewhere who had access to a *20/20 Vision* receiver would pick one up. Quite by chance I made contact with Hope who was also reaching out in desperation to try to save her people too. Lucy merely followed in my footsteps, as I'd always thought she would.'

'You wanted her to try to reach Hope?'

'Not necessarily, but I wasn't surprised that she took the chance. She was a very determined young woman.'

'*You messed with her head that's what you did and that's why she died,*' thought Anna bitterly. In that instance she loathed him. But something warned her this was not the time to challenge Jude and that it would be wiser to hold her tongue, at least for now.

'What happens when Hope and her people get here?'

'We welcome them of course. They will be absorbed into our homes for the winter and in the spring we will look to rehouse them into new accommodation. They will bring tents and livestock, knowledge that we do not have. Hope was a great lover of Nature and a tremendous botanist and healer. She also has considerable technical expertise. She will doubtless be able to pass on skills and information that will enable us together to make far better use of our resources here.'

Anna was starting to understand why Jude was so committed to this plan.

'But I thought you said Hope has a very different way of thinking from you about what help and resources people that are vulnerable or can't give back can expect,' she said. 'How do you ever see those differences working out between the two of you?'

Jude made his way over to the window and watched the busyness of the early morning movements of the Community as people went about their daily chores.

'It will not be easy,' he said. 'Hope can be very persuasive. Our people must be ready to make the arguments, to demonstrate that we are not uncaring, simply practical, dealing with a difficult situation in the best way that we can. Once these refugees join us the balance in the Community as a whole will be altered. If we are able to integrate and reproduce children successfully then we will be stronger. If we are not, and we find ourselves over burdened, then our choices are even more limited than they are now. Perhaps it is then and only then that people will finally understand the necessity of Duty Calls.'

December 31st 2099

Just as dusk was rolling in from the west, Hope and her people arrived. It was a crisp, clear night, still and bright with stars. Gathered on the mainland at the entrance to the causeway, their burning torches and raspberry coloured banners were easily visible from the island, fluttering in the light breeze. Word of their arrival spread like wildfire across the Community and everyone flocked to the shoreline in eager anticipation. So this was what their Chief Steward had planned for their new century celebrations. How incredible he was. No one had guessed.

Once the causeway had cleared they started across. In the tales that those who witnessed it told in the years to come they described a caravan of love filled with music and laughter. There were horses and cattle, sheep and pigs, people of all ages, some fit and healthy, others with obvious physical needs. They were dressed in every conceivable colour, drummers and dancers, wagons laden with furs and cages of chickens and cured meat and fish, fruits and vegetables tumbling in messy disarray.

Riding at the front, perched astride a white pony was a tiny woman, pure silver hair reaching down almost to her waist, piercing blue eyes, carrying a flaming torch as she led the procession between the two sides of the receding tide. She was flanked by young men on stout ponies, every one resplendent in furs and feathers, cloaks made of woven ribbon and coloured wools tied round their necks and laying over their mounts like saddle blankets.

The entire Community gathered to meet them. The previous week had been one of tense anticipation with no one but Anna knowing what to expect. And even she could not have imagined the spectacle of every shade of humanity that appeared over the horizon, lit up from behind by the setting sun.

As Hope's horse stepped off the causeway and onto the shore, she drew on the reins and swung herself down slowly but with the ease of an experienced rider. Jude came forward and the two cousins stood for a moment absorbing every inch of each other from top to toe. Then Hope reached out both hands and they stepped forward into each other's arms.

'I see you Jude.'

'I see you Hope.'

It was a very special moment and everyone present erupted with cheers of delight.

The celebrations stretched well into the early hours of the morning. Initially hesitant, the members of the island Community peered curiously at the sea of men, women and children that stood in mismatched ranks and files in front of them. Their simple costumes appeared in sharp contrast to those of the new arrivals, their manners more formal and less spontaneous.

But as the night wore on they shared the food and drink brought by hosts and guests alike around fires that burnt brightly up and down the beach. The barriers of unfamiliarity started to come down. Little knots began to form as children fingered curiously at beads and feathers, stroked the horses, marvelling at the workmanship of the clothing and harnesses. Older folk mingled with young ones, men with women, boys with girls, stories were exchanged and memories relived.

Just before midnight Jude and Hope led the way through the village and out along the path to the Castle. A huge bonfire smouldered in the main courtyard and they all, almost 800 people, gathered around it, blending into one in the flickering shadows of its flames.

The two leaders made their way up some steps in the centre of the huge space and stood side by side surveying the crowd. Everyone stamped their feet and banged or rattled whatever they had to hand, the ground trembling beneath them.

After a few moments Jude raised his hand and the crowd came to stillness. His voice echoed around the chamber. It was a natural amphitheatre, everyone was pin drop silent, not wishing to miss a single syllable.

'You are most welcome, each and every one of you, on this momentous evening. Our Community salutes you, Hope, and your people. You have made a long physical journey to join us, but that is as nothing compared to the distance we have all had to travel emotionally and psychologically to reach this point. And we have an even longer journey ahead. Tonight we focus on celebration, for tomorrow our work truly begins. But first, Anna.'

He waved Anna forward and she took the stage. Looking round she could see that all eyes were on her and a sudden tightness in her throat threatened to silence her. But she managed to breathe deeply and to focus on the moment as she had promised herself she would. This after all was not for her, this was for Lucy.

'Thank you. What I am about to read to you is our story. My niece created it before she died from the work that Jude's and Hope's two fathers produced with their *20/20 Vision* team. You will be very familiar with much of it, for it is our shared history.'

In a clear voice Anna then proceeded to read the first part of the document that Lucy had sent to Hope just a few weeks before, describing what Nick and Isaac had been trying to do when they had created the archive. When she got to the section headed 'Our Community' she paused. Jude had deleted the words that Lucy had written for they challenged the Duty Calls concepts that were so dear to him. The story instead now explained the tensions they faced as two Communities coming together because of the lack of resources and the need for the kinds of sacrifice that Jude had always wanted. Anna had argued with him and struggled with the concepts, knowing that Lucy had fought hard to challenge Jude too. In the end he had persuaded her that there were no alternatives and she had finally and reluctantly been worn down and agreed to fall into line.

But, as she stood in the cold night air, below a canopy of stars on the cusp of the new century Anna was faced with the reality of Jude's Duty Calls message, what it had meant for Erin, for Lucy and Seb and what, one day, it would mean for her and everyone stood before her and those to come. She saw the expectant faces waiting to be led and she suddenly realised that this was not Jude's moment, it was hers.

And in that instant Anna found a voice she didn't know she had. Closing the book in her hand containing the words she had agreed to say, she instead spoke from a place deep within herself that she had never visited before.

'Tonight something very special is taking place. Two Communities are becoming one. And this Community is not mine or yours any more. It is ours. We have the chance to transform and become something else, something new, that we can only create together. We can speculate about what that something new will be like. And we will remind ourselves that some things will never change. Every one of us will still have the gift of life and the ability to love and be loved in return. Tonight though we have a chance to start again, to use the best of what we are, build on that and adapt to the new circumstances in which we find ourselves, but in a way that we all believe in, that we can commit to together. That is my hope for the new century, my *20/20 Vision.*'

There was a moment's pause, an expectant hush and then the whole crowd stood, as one. Anna swayed slightly, overwhelmed by the tide of emotion she could sense emanating from all around her and coming in waves through the people.

From the corner of her eye she saw Hope step forward. She wrapped one arm round Anna's waist, raised her other heavenwards and without hesitation and in a clear, pure voice, started to sing.

In an instant the whole audience joined her. It was a song from the old days, an anthem that spoke of forgiveness, reconciliation, ties that bind. It was resonant with memory and meaning for everyone there. The music flowed and cascaded over them as they became a choir of one voice, a channel for all the emotions, the hopes and dreams, the stories each of them held in their hearts.

When the music ended everyone cheered and hugged and danced. Anna looked across to Jude who was standing just a few feet from her. He had pulled the hood of his robe over his head and was looking forward into the crowd. She stepped forward slightly so she could see his face.

In that instant he gave her a look. The feeling he communicated was something she had never experienced before and she recoiled as if pierced through by cold steel. Hope felt her stumble, tightened her grip on Anna's arm and looked across, but it had passed in an instant. In fact Anna could not even be certain of what she had seen. Jude lowered his hood and smiled round benignly, waving to the crowd. It was like it had never happened.

By now dawn was beginning to break and people were starting to make their way back to their various places of rest, each taking with them new friends for whom they would provide warmth and shelter for the coming few months until the spring when fresh accommodation could be created.

Eventually there was only Hope, Jude and Anna left. A young man stood patiently holding the reins of Hope's pony. He was about Seb's age, but much fairer in complexion, with clear blue eyes and thick blond hair falling over his forehead.

'My grandson, Jake,' said Hope introducing him to them both with real pride in her voice. 'His mother died when he was born and he has been with me ever since.'

Anna recognised the closeness between them instantly. It was much like the relationship she and Seb had known. The young man carried himself with humility but the quiet confidence of someone born to greatness.

'Welcome Jake, she said. 'If you would like it, you are very welcome to sleep tonight in what was my son's room. I would be honoured to have you with me.'

Glancing across at his grandmother for reassurance Jake smiled readily. 'My own room! I thank you.'

'And Hope, my niece's cottage is available for you, if you would feel happy there? We would be next door to each other.'

Hope wrapped her in a warm embrace. 'How very kind you are, Anna.'

So it was agreed in an instant. Jude had stood quietly while these arrangements were being agreed and the four fell into step as they made their way back towards the village. When they reached his cottage he pleaded tiredness, and barely looking at Anna, bade them all goodnight and went inside, closing the door behind him. They walked on and Anna showed them both where they would be sleeping, promising to answer any questions in the morning.

She was so tired when she finally climbed into bed that she could hardly keep her eyes open and certainly had no energy to ponder on the night's events. She fell almost instantly to sleep with Lela curled at her feet as usual. In her hand was a silver necklace that normally hung round her neck. It bore a picture of an oak tree and two words: *Grow Strong.*

The Reconciliation

It was a hard, bleak winter. The new arrivals took their places in the various barns and cottages where spaces had managed to be found and began the journey of gradually learning to adapt to the customs and practices of the Community. They were grateful to their hosts and showed this by sharing anything they had. And it soon became apparent that it was not just food and livestock and transport and utensils that they had brought. They also came with joy.

They had been unaware that there existed people and cultures that were so different from each other, but it was obvious from the start that they were. Anna saw it in the differences in the ways they each behaved, paid attention and had time, even for the weakest amongst them. She spoke to Hope about it.

'Lucy saw how the *20/20 Vision* archive captured the everyday ways of being, the things that were so familiar back then that no one really noticed but to her appeared extraordinary and wonderful. That same recognition of difference is happening before my eyes now. I can't believe how much variety there is in each of our Communities and the diversity in what we each choose to prioritise and give attention to,' she mused.

Hope smiled. 'We can all be focused when we have found something that we are motivated to do because it matters to us. I am often struck by the energy and effort that we will give to those activities and people about whom we feel passionate. Once you know what someone loves it isn't hard to persuade them to find the energy to follow that dream.'

'I guess we're all different.'

'That's right. And we can be thankful for that!'

They were working in Anna's cottage alone. In the week or so that they had been together Jake had become increasingly active in the Community and had today joined the other young men taking fodder to the livestock that were gathered close into the village for the winter. The two women were preparing what would be the evening meal. It had become something of a routine to bake, cook and eat together. Hope was an expert with herbs and spices and had managed to introduce new flavours and depths of deliciousness into their cooking that Anna could only have dreamed of before.

'I was brought up to like the idea of accepting and embracing difference. Whenever my father Nick forgot a chore or didn't do something to my mother's exacting standards he used to say to her that he couldn't be good at everything,' laughed Hope. You know my mother and Jude's father Isaac were brother and sister don't you?'

'Yes, I did know that.'

'Jude had quite a tough upbringing I think.'

'How do you mean?'

'Well, Isaac was a bit of a hard taskmaster to be honest. I don't think he had much time for Jude, or his wife for that matter. My father used to mutter about it all the time. He didn't like the way Isaac treated his sister.'

'Jude's mother was Nick's sister?'

'She was. It was all a bit incestuous actually. Nick and Isaac were students together. They each had a sister, they all met up one holiday and the rest, as they say, is history. The two men had very similar political interests but different views about the best way to take them forward.'

'I know. Lucy found out quite a bit about those when she was doing her research for the story she wrote.'

'I wanted to ask you about that. Did you read out everything she wrote at the ceremony at New Year?'

'No, Jude changed her version. But when it came to it I just couldn't say the words he had given me. I don't know what came over me. I think he was furious.'

'Why?'

Anna thought for a moment.

'Probably lots of reasons. We'd worked on a version of the story that explained why he felt we needed to follow his Duty Calls arrangements once the two Communities came together. I'd taken a lot of persuading, but in the end I'd fallen into line and promised to read what he wanted me to say.'

'Ah yes, he's told me about those Duty Calls ideas. He knows what I think about them.'

Anna focused on peeling potatoes, and spoke in a barely audible whisper.

'Lucy hated Duty Calls. She and Seb decided they'd rather die than live under those rules. When it came to it, it just felt like I'd have been betraying them if I'd said those words.'

The two women fell silent.

'It must have been terrible for you to lose them both.'

'It was. It still is. When I read her message to you I felt so guilty for not seeing it coming.'

'What message?'

'The story she sent you and those last words she wrote about her right to choose whether to live or die. If I'd seen them sooner I might have been able to change their minds.'

Hope stopped what she was doing. 'You think that was Lucy's suicide note?' she asked.

'I just wish I'd seen it in time.'

Hope looked thoughtful. 'You knew Lucy so well, but from what you've told me of her she was full of life and determination, not desperation. I must confess, Anna, I didn't read despair in those words of Lucy's. I read challenge and conviction, victory even.'

They carried on working, each turning over their thoughts. Once the stew was prepared Hope made them each herb tea. They wrapped blankets around their shoulders and sat outside to catch the late afternoon sunshine while they drank it.

'What was Jude like when he was young?' asked Anna.

'He was quite a sad child I think, rather lonely and isolated. I was not a good cousin or friend I'm afraid. In fact I was rather selfish and neglectful towards him, getting on with my own life and leaving him out more than I should have done. He used to seem rather on the outside. He was studious yes, and always trying to join in, but wistful.'

'If I can, I'd like to make up for my thoughtlessness during whatever time I have left with him now. I was so lucky. My parents and I were very close, there was love and laughter in abundance in our home and I had grandparents that adored me. I think I reminded them of Mia a little. Friendships and acceptance just came easily to me, whereas Jude struggled to belong.'

'And Isaac didn't help. He was quite a harsh and judgemental character; I was scared of him when I was a child. Nothing Jude did was ever good enough. And his mother was lonely too I think and probably turned to her son more than she should have done for support. Jude was dutiful of course, as you can imagine, but when I think back he probably felt jealous and maybe angry too, though with no one to talk to those feelings may have been hidden to him: a blind spot if you like. I would have felt the same if I'd have been in his shoes.'

'Families eh?' smiled Anna. 'They've a lot to answer for.'

'Nature versus nurture I suppose. Which side are you on?'

Anna had set to work laying the table.

'Well, I've never been too sure on that one to be honest. Before I had Seb I'd have said it was all down to the way we bring them up. But he was so like his Dad and completely different from Lucy, in spite of them being cousins and so close in age and experience. I guess at the end of the day it's always going to be a bit of each.'

'I'm sure you're right,' said Hope. 'But I do think what parents do is important, especially when we're very young. The less you feel safe or like you can trust whoever cares for you when you are a child, the more anxious and alert you're likely to become. Jude was always inclined to see risks and dangers in situations whereas I always saw adventure and opportunity. And that perception of the world tended to hold him back, make him nervous about taking chances. To be honest with you, I was really surprised when I found out that he held such a leadership position here.'

'Why?'

'Because this is such a risky situation and Jude would always want to do right by you all and protect you from danger. That sense of feeling threatened but also responsible is not a great combination for anyone's feelings of well being. And when you are the leader, you're in a lonely position. Who does he turn to: God? I wouldn't be surprised if he is constantly stressed. Have you seen his nails? They are chewed down to the quick.'

At that moment the door to the cottage opened and Jake entered, back from the day's work. He unwound a thick woollen scarf and shrugged off his jacket, making his way immediately to the fire and warming himself at the grate.

'Good day?' asked Anna.

'Very good, thank you,' he replied. 'We got all the animals fed and watered safely by mid afternoon and then they took me down to meet the children in the cottage in the village centre.'

'I'm glad you've been there,' said Anna. 'Did you meet Scarlett and the other girls?'

'I did. She showed me round. It was wonderful to see healthy little girls playing happily as well as boys. Scarlett's so good with them.'

The evening passed in conversation and laughter, stories were exchanged and appetites appeased. Jake asked a lot of questions, particularly about Scarlett who had clearly made an impression on him. Hardly surprising, she was fearless and determined as well as being extraordinarily beautiful, tall and slender with smooth olive skin and deep brown eyes that could flash with emotion one second and dance with delight the next. The two women exchanged knowing looks and when he got up to clear the table Hope winked broadly at Anna behind his back. They knew a romance in the offing when they saw it.

Eventually Hope announced it was time for her to turn in and she left to go to her bed in Lucy's cottage. Anna and Jake settled in chairs on either side of the fireplace, enjoying each other's company in front of the last of the embers in a way that was a bitter sweet reminiscence to her of when Seb had been alive. Anna glanced across at him as he concentrated on polishing and cleaning the tools he had gathered to use around the cottage and beyond. She smiled to herself. It would be wonderful if Scarlett and he were to be able to reach out to each other in love and one day join the two Communities together.

Yawning, she said her goodnights and went through to her room. Blowing out the candle she snuggled down under the warm blankets. As she started to drift towards sleep her mind went back to Lucy and Seb. She could still not believe they were truly gone. She tried to remember exactly what she had read when Jude showed her the message Lucy had sent on the night she died. Hope's words had sown a seed of doubt in her mind that she had never expected. She couldn't deny it had seemed incredible at the time that they should take such drastic action, but what other possible explanation could there be?

The Transformation

The next few months saw a growing closeness and mutual understanding and respect develop between the two groups. Hope kept her promise and showed constant kindness and patience to Jude. They sat and walked together every day, Jude talking, Hope listening and only occasionally putting a question about his Duty Calls beliefs in a way that helped him to reflect and consider, not become defensive or arrogant. The growing affection they had for each other was very evident. Anna asked her about it one day.

'Would you say Jude and you are close?'

'Jude's probably been surrounded by people but very lonely his whole life,' Hope responded. 'I hadn't appreciated quite how much he had lived in his own thoughts until we began the correspondence last year when we first connected through *20/20 Vision.* He needed that distance, using the laptop to communicate gave him the space to open up about his reasons for believing in Duty Calls.'

'But to be honest we talked less about those philosophies and more about our shared story, the challenges we both experienced as fallible human beings that each of our Communities looked to for guidance and wisdom. Jude, I think, became more and more aware of the voice in his head that told him he wasn't good enough and caused him to strive harder and harder every day. It was the voice of a critical parent, a script that he'd been given from his earliest years. I tried to redress the balance a little, yes to help him to work hard, but to see the decisions and behaviours he found difficult to deliver in the context of the limitations we all have. I don't know if I succeeded in helping him to be less critical of himself, habits are difficult to break after all and he has had many years of listening to those inner voices. But I tried.'

She looked thoughtful. 'Perhaps the conversations we had over the airways happened in a way that gave Jude a certain anonymity and freedom to express himself that his day to day existence and role did not allow. It perhaps helped that I didn't see him as a high ranking figure. To me he was just my cousin, someone on the same level I suppose. Jude and I have history and a different relationship and responsibilities towards each other.'

'And I am not blameless in all this you know, Anna. I contributed to his feelings of isolation by leaving him out when we were young. I owe him something for that. Over the months I gained an insight into Jude that opened my eyes to who he truly is and why. And I like to think I helped him to do the same. I suppose I walked a little way in his shoes.'

As winter turned to spring there was a growing contrast evident between the new life of green shoots emerging from the earth and Hope's increasing frailty. As she grew weaker they ate their meals together round her bed each day. Jake rarely left her side, spending long hours reading to her from an ancient book of poems that she loved and kept under her pillow. They moved her bed to the window so she could see out across the fields to the sea. Between him and Anna they managed a succession of visitors, both from her own Community and those that were now proud to call themselves a part of the one family they were all becoming.

Eventually it was clear that the end was near. Anna called for Jude who came instantly. He had been to the cottage himself every day and had sat with her, often just holding her hand as she slept. He was transformed in her presence. Anna was sure that Lucy would never have been able to believe that this side of him existed.

In the last hours of her life Jake sat on one side, Jude on the other. Anna hovered at the end of the bed, watching all three of them, ready to respond if needed.

'I wasn't kind to you, Jude. I am sorry for my past selfishness,' Hope murmured.

He was overwhelmed. 'It is not you who is not kind, it is me,' he said.

'You have been a good and faithful servant to the Community, Jude.'

'I wish that were true. I have been anything but.'

'That is your father's voice speaking, don't listen to him, Jude. You are too hard on yourself, cousin. We are all works in progress, simply fragile beings striving to do what we know to be right against a background where so much is making us choose what is wrong. You have done your best. No one can ask more.'

Jude was sobbing. 'I wish that were true. I have sinned, Hope.'

'None of us is perfect. There is a way for you to feel good again. Have faith, Jude. Stop striving so hard and try to be a little kinder to yourself. Trust that you are good enough. We all find our own way in the end.'

Those were the last words she spoke. The three of them kept vigil by her bedside all night. Each breath came more slowly from her body until finally there was one last deep sigh. They each sensed that her spirit, her strength and wisdom, inspiration and energy had passed away. She was no more.

The Confession

The funeral, as had always been the custom in Hope's Community, took place the next day. A pyre was quickly constructed in the middle of the causeway and her body lain on it. Everyone watched from the shoreline as it burnt away, flames reaching high up into the sky and licking round the husk of her. Eventually just a few remnants were swept out into the sea by the incoming tide. Candles were lit and as dusk rolled in they sang the songs of separation and farewell that they had known all their lives.

Anna stood between Jake and Jude, all three of them lost in their thoughts and memories of a woman so dear to each of them. Then it was over and the sea extinguished the last of the flames.

Jake turned into the village and stood, surrounded by the other young people, all of whom were trying to find words and ways to comfort him. Scarlett was at his side and as Anna watched them she saw her reach for his hand and hold him close. He sobbed silently into her shoulder as she wrapped him in her arms to contain and share all that he was feeling. Anna felt huge tenderness for them both. She sensed they would be safe together.

Jude however was inconsolable. Tears were pouring down his face and he could barely walk. At first she had seen this grieving as to be expected, but there was something different about it, something that unsettled her and left her concerned for him. She managed to keep him in the shadows as the crowd dispersed, though she was aware of a few curious looks that were thrown at them by those who caught his reaction. She expected that everyone would just recognise that although he was their leader, he was human just like everyone else.

'Do you want me to come back with you?' she asked, casting troubled eyes over his face. 'You maybe don't want to be alone tonight?'

By now everyone had disappeared and the lanes were quiet once again. Jude turned to Anna, his eyes vacant and unseeing. She was really worried now, for she had never seen him like this. He started to walk and headed in the direction of the church, but instead veered off along the path towards the Castle. She hurried to keep up with him, Lela at her heels.

When they reached the gateway he paused and looked about him till he found the brass plaque he had shown Lucy less than a year ago, nailed high up on one of the walls. He stood looking at it for some time, then without warning wrenched it from its place and threw it to the ground.

'What's wrong Jude? What's the matter? Let me take you home. You're exhausted.'

He ignored her and instead made his way into the main courtyard, the scene of the New Year's Eve celebrations. He stood looking around, appearing to be lost in thought. It was very dark now. There was no moon tonight and thick clouds blocked out any stars.

'Jude, please, it's late. We need to get back.'

He turned and for the first time appeared to become aware of her presence.

'I cannot go back, Anna. It is too late for that. Look,' he raised his fist with his thumb upright and turned towards the west where the last glimmers of the sun were visible. 'I once showed this to Lucy. From here I can block out the entire village. We are tiny, inconsequential in history. We will all be forgotten one day.'

Now she was becoming really worried. This was not the Jude she recognised at all. He turned and half stumbled, half ran further into the Castle area, and out towards the other side of the hill on which it stood, where the walls opened onto the sheer cliffs that fell away into the rolling sea now crashing against the rocks below.

Anna chased after him, Lela racing ahead, sensing there was something amiss, and trying to herd Jude back. He came to the end of the path and stopped as close to the cliff edge as it was possible to be. In the nick of time Anna grabbed Lela and held her tight to stop her from moving forward any further. She could hear the gravel sliding away under Jude's feet. He fell to his knees.

'Come away from the edge Jude, please, it's too dangerous,' she shouted.

He stayed where he was, a silent figure barely distinguishable in the darkness. Anna edged closer so she could speak more quietly. He was in such pain. She just wanted to help him.

'Come Jude, I know you're upset, we all are. But Hope wouldn't have wanted you to feel like this. She wanted you to carry on, to lead us, to be happy.'

Slowly Jude turned to look at her.

'You don't understand Anna. None of you do.'

'Don't understand what?'

'I don't deserve to be happy.'

Anna knew she had to find the right words. It reminded her of when she was trying to talk to Lucy. Not for the first time she found herself wondering: *What would Erin have said?'*

'Remember Hope's words to you, Jude. None of us is perfect. We all make mistakes.'

He gave no reaction, but got slowly to his feet. Lela was on the ground, edging towards him, exactly as she would if she were trying to round up a wayward sheep. Jude did something Anna had not expected. He threw back his head and laughed.

'Mistakes, Anna? Mistakes? You have no idea. Mistakes can be forgiven, overlooked perhaps, understood. But sins? I don't think so. What would you do about sins?'

'I don't know what you mean, Jude. Come away from the edge and we can talk about this. I'm sure we can work things out.'

He stood completely still and faced her. They were just a pace or two apart. For an instant she thought he was going to step forward and pull her towards him. Instead he clasped his hands together in front of his chest. When he spoke next it was in the calm and decisive voice of the Chief Steward that she recognised of old.

'What did your mother used to say, Anna? *The saddest words ever are if only, but too late.* I must confess to you, for I have done something that cannot be undone but that I regret with every ounce of my being. I have sinned.'

And with that he told her. And as she screamed and lunged forward to claw his eyes from his face, he stepped backwards and, arms outstretched, spiralled and plummeted like a huge black bat into the rocks below.

Five years later

'Come on Cait, eat up. It's time to go.'

Scarlett waited patiently while the child finished her biscuit and milk and then expertly wiped her mouth and hands while at the same time pushing the rest of the breakfast crockery into the sink to be washed. It was a familiar routine, one they repeated every morning, before hurrying along to the village square where Cait joined the other young children and Scarlett, heavily pregnant, carried out her childcare duties for the rest of the Community.

She gave a quick glance round the cottage that had once belonged to Lucy but was now home to her, Jake and their soon to be added to family. They had moved in just before Cait's birth and she'd loved playing house, making a home for them. They knew the building's history, but that had only made her even more determined to bring laughter and love back into its walls. She felt she had succeeded for they both often said as they settled down to sleep in each other's arms every night that they had never been happier.

And when Cait was born, whole and healthy, their happiness was complete. She was the first of many now, children created through the joining of flesh of two communities, each bringing renewed optimism and vigour to the island and reinforcing that they were indeed so much stronger together.

Mother and child walked hand in hand through the streets greeting friends and neighbours all moving purposefully about their business but seemingly enjoying the expectation of the day ahead.

Jake had left some time before on an early morning fishing trip that they expected would bring fresh mackerel into the larders and give them enough to smoke and store to see them through another winter.

She hummed to herself as she swung her hips, weighed down by the new life that would soon spring from her. It was a boy this time, she was certain of it and she had already named him in her head. Stephen. It had been Lucy's grandfather's name. Whenever Anna told stories of him her eyes lit up at the fond memories she carried in her head. He sounded a real character, strongly protective of his family, a calm presence but full of fun and vitality. That was the kind of man she wanted her son to be. She liked the idea of a child living in the house bearing a name that Lucy would have known and loved.

There was no doubting Anna's delight at the idea. She was like a grandmother to Cait, dropping in to see her every day, always available to watch over her if the need arose. She would regularly rock her to sleep with stories of the island, weaving tales of good and evil, arising from their shared history. Her tales were magical. Sometimes they told of danger to threaten them from bogey man Jude. But always there were stories of safety and protection from Hope who brought compassion and healing to the vulnerable and weary. Like the other children, through these reminiscences woven together from memories and events, each developed their sense of who they were, where they came from, and their heritage. Hope's memory lived on through these tales and Anna could only guess at the impact of the bloodline from such a woman to this young child and beyond.

As leader, Anna had done her best to take the learning she had received and use it to shape the new Community into something stronger than before, capable of outlasting and sustaining generations to come. One of her first actions had been to establish a council of twelve chosen from the Community as a whole. They acted as her true friends, providing support but also challenge to help her to steer her way through the difficult choices she often had to make.

One of their first decisions concerned the laptop, locked away in the crypt. In the end they decided that they all should have the chance to use it, to learn about their past and build ideas for the future, and that everyone being able to access it once a year would be the Community's birthday present to each person that lived on the island. But Anna was mindful of Jude's warnings. It was not to be used again to send signals to try to reach other communities. They had been fortunate with Hope, there was no way of knowing what any others that might have listened in to past signalling would be like and they all agreed that it was their first duty to protect their own.

One season followed another and a simple rhythm had begun to settle over the families. For Scarlett and Jake this had started to define their existence, given them seeds of confidence to begin to plan for a future for themselves and their children. They knew that no one could look too far ahead, but as each year ticked by and the

Community became more confident in its strength and wisdom, skills and experience so everyone, deep down, dared to hope.

Scarlett and Cait were almost at their destination when they heard the sound of running footsteps. Turning they saw Fin. He could hardly speak with the effort he had made to race towards them.

'Ships, Scarlett! There's ships!'

For an instant Scarlett assumed he must mean the boats that had gone out fishing that morning. But he shook his head.

'No, big ships. There's sails. Come and look.'

And he grabbed her hand and pulled her as fast as he could through the cottages and out onto to the shoreline.

There were already half a dozen villagers gathered and more were coming from all directions. Scarlett shielded her eyes as she looked towards the east where the sun was making its way above the horizon.

There were ships.

She counted six. They were coming fast towards them, sails unfurled in the breeze, making straight for the beach below the Castle.

'Someone send for Anna,' she shouted.

'I'm here,' called a voice and in that instant Anna came round the corner, followed shortly afterwards by Jake and the rest of the fishing party.

'We turned back when we saw them,' said Jake. 'Who can they be do you think?'

'They're coming from the north,' said Scarlett. 'Maybe somewhere like Scandinavia.'

'It's possible. That was one of the places that Hope always suspected a Community might survive.'

The news spread like wildfire and within half an hour almost everyone was gathered on the shoreline watching the boats coming towards them. They looked large enough to carry about fifty people each, but as they approached Scarlett could start to count heads and they each looked half empty. Although there were oars stowed along each side, they were relying on the stiff breeze to carry them forward.

They watched, mesmerised, as the sails drew closer. Eventually the foremost came to within a few metres and dropped anchor before it might run aground. The other five did the same. They were identical, narrow and fast being skilfully manoeuvred by those on board.

And then as they watched, each ship as one disgorged its occupants into the surf. All men. They waded forward up the gently shelving shingle till they stood shoulder to shoulder along the beach. There were probably around 200 in total.

Anna stood at the head of the Community, flanked on one side by Jake, the other Scarlett who was holding Cait's hand. Everyone else stood in mixed groups, men, women and children all dumbfounded by the sight. Anna stepped forward and raised both arms.

'Greetings.'

One of the men from the first boat took a few steps towards her, then stopped. He was taller than the others and although, like them, he was dressed in leather and fur he had an air of authority that instantly identified him as their leader.

He surveyed the crowd carefully, appearing to take in every single person that was there. His eyes lingered on Scarlett's belly and she could feel the rest of the men following his gaze. She felt the child inside her turn over and kick her so hard that she involuntarily winced and put her hand to her stomach. Suddenly, she was terrified.

The man raised his hand. He was clutching a red silk scarf which he held high in the air. It fluttered and waved in the breeze. There was a momentary pause. When he could be sure that all eyes were upon him he dropped his arm to his side.

At this signal every one of the men reached into his jacket.

It was over in seconds. Jake was the first to step forward. The bullet passed through his skull at his forehead and he dropped to his knees and forward into the sand where he lay. Anna, arms still raised, turned on her heels to face her people and standing firm screamed one word. They obeyed. They ran.

The men scythed through them like corn. It was clear what they were after. Half grabbed the young women and older girls, throwing them to the ground and tying them swiftly with ropes they pulled from round their waists. The rest picked off any man that came after them, leaving thirty or so bodies weeping great waves of redness into the sand and surf.

Scarlett acted on instinct. Grabbing Cait she turned and put as much distance between themselves and the sea as she could. Stumbling and staggering she managed to get them both to the shelter of one of the huts and here she stopped and turned, panting, to see what was happening. Almost instantly she reached for Cait and pulled her face into her body so she could not witness the carnage being acted out before her.

The men were half dragging, half carrying thirty or so women towards the boats. When they reached the sea they held their heads under till they were half drowned, then dragged them out into the water and threw them unceremoniously into the crafts. As she watched they were quickly tied to the sides and then the boats were turned expertly with their oars and they made their way as quickly as they had come out into the open sea.

The man who had given the signal still stood on the beach. Anna walked up to him. She appeared to show no fear. Scarlett was transfixed.

'Why have you done this?'

He looked her up and down. She was well past child bearing years so no use to him, alive or dead. But he admired her courage.

'We will be back for more.'

And with that he turned and waded out into the surf, swinging himself up into the final remaining canoe. All they could hear was the screaming of the women piercing the air as the boats disappeared into the distance.

Starting Over

When she looked back, Scarlett could barely remember what followed. The next few days passed in a blur. It was as if she had closed off from the pain and was being allowed to deal only a drop at a time with all that she felt. She often wondered later if this numbness had evolved as Nature's way of saving them from themselves. She suspected if it had not been for her responsibilities to Cait and the knowledge of the new life she carried inside her she would have stayed where she had dropped down into the sand and never got up again.

As it was, the Community moved as one, sharing the human experiences of loss, disbelief, anger and despair. The funerals, the reality of the trauma, failed to bring acceptance but they at least created a visual memory that they all experienced of the bodies of their loved ones being laid to rest in a ceremony held in the centre of the Castle. All of the names were chiselled into a memorial stone that stood bearing witness to their place in the history of the Community.

When it was over and everyone had placed their tokens of respect and love on the turf covered mounds dotted across the central courtyard, Anna came forward to speak. She gave a simple eulogy, managing to recreate the essence of each of the individuals that had been lost to what was, as she reminded them all, one collective family. When she came to Jake her eyes rested momentarily on Scarlett and Cait, filled with compassion as they wept their silent tears. In the moment that followed, broken only by the sound of the wind rustling through grass and seabirds calling high above them, everyone present made their own contribution to the single prayer that soared and bore these loved ones into an eternal remembrance.

Then Anna rested both her hands on the memorial. Her shoulders low, she paused to catch her breath and gather her thoughts. When she lifted her face to look around at the people, her eyes shone bright with tears.

'Never have we had to face such an event. But we are a Community and I promise we will survive. I am your leader. My duty is to create the conditions to protect us all. What choices do we have? There are not many.'

She raised her hand and counted one by one on her fingers as she spoke.

'We could rally what is left of us, fortify the Castle and try to withstand any future attacks. But how difficult would that be to sustain and, even if we did, there are no guarantees we could survive another episode like the one we have suffered. We would always be living in fear, ever watchful for the next battle, directing what few resources we have into defence, not productivity.'

'Or we could take our chances and run and hide, try to re-establish ourselves somewhere new. But the recent outrage has left the balance of the Community changed. We have lost a significant part of our strength and resource and we have too few of us left to save the weakest and those most frail who remain.'

She held up her third finger.

211

'We have only one choice and in our hearts I suspect we all know what we have to do.'

She paused, just long enough for everyone to see the answer for themselves rather than need to be told.

'The fittest amongst us have to leave and take their chances. The rest of us will remain and take ours.'

Epilogue

They were packed and ready in a matter of days. Scarlett led the way in the early morning mist, riding side saddle on a stout pony, Cait sat on one next to her in front of Fin, already a confident little rider, his arms wrapped tightly round her. In total there were around 500 of them, dragging carts filled with as many of the necessities for re-establishing themselves as they could muster. At least some knew the way. The destination was Hope's old homeland that some of them had left only a few years earlier, a place that held memories for many of family and friends, a Community that had been dying for the want of fertile women like the one for which the invaders had stolen their women. The irony was not lost on Scarlett. Jake too had gone hunting, now his people were simply taking back what they had also come to find.

Anna watched them leave. She and the other remnants stood till the tide had turned fully, covering the causeway as it did every day and every night. Eventually they drifted away, back to the various cottages and places that each of them called home. This would be a new and very different day.

She stood in the courtyard of their two cottages, and as she glanced around she allowed her mind to replay some old scenes. Lucy jumping into the cart filled with optimism as they left for the lighthouse, Seb comforting them and helping to bring Sam's body to the churchyard, the morning she had crossed into the cottage to find them locked together in death, the night Hope and Jake had first come to stay.

Pushing open the door of what had once been Lucy's, then Scarlett and Jake's home, Anna stood on the threshold for a moment looking round the room, images of scenes that she had witnessed there flashing through her mind's eye. There was little left apart from the bare furniture. But on the table there was something she recognised. It was the poetry book that Hope had kept under her pillow from which Jake had read to her every day.

Crossing to it, she laid her hand on the book, recognising this had last been held by someone she had loved. Closing her eyes she reached out to her friend through its pages and in that connection felt a moment's solace and comfort.

She picked it up and flicked through. As she did so a piece of folded paper, slipped between the leaves, fell out. Her name was on it. She recognised Hope's writing instantly and, crossing to the window, she unfolded the paper. Breathing a sigh of gratitude, in the first rays of dawn she read the message that had been left for her.

My dear friend

And so it goes. History tells us it is hard to hope, that human kind will always snatch those resources to which we believe we are entitled. Feelings of entitlement too often stretch to anything that we can take from those we think of as 'different' to preserve those we perceive as 'our own'.

Dare we justify such behaviour as the instinct of survivors? What of fairness? What of love?

There may come a time when justice sweeps like a tsunami to victory, but we cannot know when that might be. In the meantime, the wicked do not appear to perish.

Perhaps we can only learn from the past and hope for the future. And rest that hope on a collective faith that love and justice will, somehow, one day rhyme.

Hope Grigori

21928733R00134

Printed in Great Britain
by Amazon